At Whitt's End

At Whitt's End

A VARIETY OF POETRY AND NARRATIVES

Janean J. Phillips

First Printing: 2014

ISBN 978-0-9971375-3-8

Photos by Diana Shrout Williams, at The Trolley Stop,
Dayton, Ohio

Illustration by Craig V. Thomas

Typefaces:
Glowist, 2014 by Flavortype
Lora, 2011 by Olga Karpushina

Printed and Published by Braughler Books
www.braughlerbooks.com

DEDICATION

This book is dedicated to all of my family and friends who have helped me and supported me along the way.

To my father, Charles, who has been so graciously patient and kind and who still loves me unconditionally.
I Thank You,
And I love you forever.

To my mother, Jane, God rest her soul, who has been besideme all of this time, who loved me unconditionally and who will forever be in my heart.
I Thank You and I love you forever.

To Craig and Marta, Claire and Josh, Aubrey and Mina, I love you more than I can ever express. I am very proud of you and I Thank You for being my "personal cheerleaders." Thank you, Craig V. Thomas, for the fantastic book cover!

A LOUD Thank You to John, Kathy, Amy, June, Diana, Chris D., Sandy, Sarah, Vickie, Viv, Barb, Amber, Grace, Jessica, CC and all of the girls who have supported me, and helped start a fantastic tradition of themed GNO and GNI's (Girls Nite Out/Girls Nite In).

We've had a blast, and will continue to dance and sing, wear boas and hats, and any old costume imaginable, drink chocolatinis, and do cartwheels, in real life, in theory, in our dreams and in our hearts. The party just keeps on going, and going. May it never die.

AT WHITT'S END

The cuckoo was up, dismal and dim, with no hope of promise,
Too early for normal human creatures to arise,
she concluded.
Achy as usual, Whitt reluctantly slithered out of bed,
Feeling quite isolated.

Her heart was pounding, for sleep she was lacking.
The water was an irritant, an unwelcome moment,
Whereas most would find this time enjoyable, she thought.

She left her domicile, dressed as much as possible,
Wrinkles on her face, wrinkles on her clothes,
A knapsack of sustenance she could not find the energy
to consume.

No greeting upon her arrival, no greeting in the place
of respite,
No address, no accommodations to speak of...
Whitt was alone, in a mass of heartbeats.

Her workspace was lacking in photos, nor of colors
Or creativity as her coworkers.
Why are they not my friends? In her lonely head, she asked...
As she sat down again, to the sounds of the droning

And the hums of the chatter of which she was not a part.
Nothing to display.

Why am I an odd individual?
Why does this incessant thinking haunt me so?
Why, in this world, do I walk alone, sleep alone, laugh alone,
eat alone...
With tender climbing and nobody playing and aches
always aching?
People lie. People cheat. People yell. People cuss.

The dogs and the cats have crapped in my garden again...
But that is what animals do.

Another frequent veil of another space and time,
She was at her breaking point.
She could not take another day, another moment of her
heart aching,
Her soul breaking, her mind exploding...so...
In that space between alive and dead,
She drenched the space with metal projectiles,
Ending everyone in their path.

It was noiseless.
It was blank.
Finally, peace in the darkness of the light.

The space cleared and Whitt was animated.
With head in the palms of her hands, elbows at her workspace,
Her vision cleared and the noise was still in existence,
The droning was louder and the humming and
chatter continued.

A hand on her shoulder. A smile from a novel, appealing male.
Whitt's eyes opened for the first time.
Her heart was pounding and it did not hurt.
An invitation.
A compliment long time coming.
An instance of oneness.
The space vanished and Whitt was no longer at her end.

I WANT TO BE SOMEONE'S ZOEY

Across from him I sat, perplexed, as the sparkle in his eyes
Continued to get brighter, by the word full.
My mind was wandering, but his voice maintained focus.
He spoke of her, as if to say that she was the next best thing
Beyond original creation.

She was delightful, full of energy and excitement,
A bit of a mystery and she was as tall as a crane.
I imagined a crane, in my mind's eye, and all I could see was
The alligator in waiting, as he pounced on her
And drug her down to the depths of her watery grave.
My focus was holding back a smirk.
He did not notice.

I found that knot in my stomach, that had been missing
Since my last conversation with him.
That knot was a good knot.
A lump generating a stir of my own excitement, giddiness,
Playfulness and hope.
This one is different, I convinced myself.

Old but new, we aimlessly continued on our path
Without being concerned too much about life,
About what others might think.

We convinced ourselves that it was the journey,
Not the destination, that mattered.

As the hourglass emptied and the sun rose and fell,
He spoke again and again of Zoey, as if she were someone
That he thought, with whom I would love to have met.
She was real. She was alive.
She was his previous love, with whom he had still kept
in contact.

My head tilted a bit each time, as we met for coffee,
As we met for living room entertainment,
As we chit-chatted about lonely things,
About past things and about nothing at all.
I felt as if my head were to tilt one more time,
I was bound to fall over...
But falling was what I did best.
It was one of my defects.

With each meeting, he continued to tell me about her.
Before our lovemaking, after lovemaking, sometimes
even during...
About her lovely eyes, her ample bosom, her giraffe neck...
I picked up on his disappointment of her youthful ranting,
ideals and spirit. I picked up on his disappointments, of
everything and everyone.

He was impervious to his own immaturity, of his faults
and of his many vices. With each setting of the moon, my
attention waned
And I fell again into a dark sadness.
He was now cold and unreachable to me.
He was another bag of bones. A lifeless human creature.
He was a bone of contention.

"I want to be someone's Zoey," I shouted, but he did
not listen.
I want to be spoken of, in that manner...
To be loved, cherished, revered, idolized and needed.
I could not get through to him, of his inconsiderate speeches,
His droning of this perfect creature to whom I could not
live up.

I corrected my defect and exited tearfully and gracefully...
Acknowledging that he was another waste of space,
time, energy.
And the hourglass continued...

PARTY WITH PRUITT

The sun rose and fell in the presence of Pruitt.
She was the one that everyone wanted to be with, to
be near, to be like.
Pruitt was a shell of a human being, happy and spicy on
the outside...
Sad and crushed on the inside.

Pruitt developed a status that she helped blossom.
She was wealthy, but never flaunted it.
She gave the biggest parties.
She knew the musicians of all the local bands.
She danced.
She shared.
She sang.
She decorated a room, when she entered it...
When she said GO, everyone WENT.

No one knew Pruitt, like Anton did.
He loved her from the moment that he first saw her.
But he did not tell her.
She was alone.
He was alone.

He stood by her side, during her breakups with friends,

with foes,
With men who were boys.
He stood by her side, when she was sick, feeding her with
love and kindness,
Time and compassion.
He stood by her side, when she would make the
wrong decisions,
Only squeaking out advice when she asked for it.

Pruitt was damaged and unhappy. She was lonely
and confused.
She was looking for something, but could not verbalize
As to what she was seeking.
She believed that she had no friends, just surface and
toxic individuals,
Who loved to take advantage of her kindness, her
natural beauty,
Her natural personality of nurturer.

So without forethought of Anton,
Her one and only true friend,
Whom she could not see,
She took her own life.
Anton was now the damaged one.
He regretted his silence and never thought of Pruitt again.

THE IN-BETWEEN GIRL AND THE BOYFRIEND CONVENTION

Spring was approaching and Maxine was now finally living
with no regrets.
It was a long time coming...
The blues had finally turned.
Spring brings hope and Maxine was first in line.

She dubbed herself the In-Between Girl.

She was in between boyfriends, and she was tired of looking.
In between dress sizes, but still hopeful,
In between homes, and downsizing was her current cure.
In between jobs, and stretching food had become an art form.
In between pets, and she missed her Fido so...
She was In Between...everything.

The wrinkles had subsided. Her baggage was lost in space.
She preferred a ring around her finger, instead of under her eyes,
But makeup was making up for lost time.

Without work, Maxine felt as if she was unproductive,
So she became a volunteer.
She was looking forward to The Home Improvement
Spring Event,

At the local convention center...
Sit-ups and push-ups, leg-lifts and aerobics had paid off
and finally...
Saturday rolled around and she was as fit as a fiddle.
She knew she looked great and was ready for anything...

While helping at 9 o'clock, she spied a thief.
It was the man who stole her heart.
While helping at 11 o'clock, she spied a criminal.
It was the man who lied under oath.
While helping at 1 o'clock, she spied a felon.
It was the man who cheated on her, twice!
While helping at 3 o'clock, she spied a prisoner.
It was the man who had her captivated.
Convict.
Lawbreaker.
Gangster.
Villain.

They all showed up, all under one roof, along with petite
female eye candy...
Maxine was livid.
None of those men had ever lifted a finger, lifted a hammer,
Lifted her spirits or even lifted themselves off of their
couches for a beer.
Maxine was now in between thoughts,

In between choices of making sense or making a scene.
She worked hard at looking good.
She worked hard at eliminating clutter.
She was a volunteer, and she was
The In-Between Girl at the Boyfriend Convention.

FOREIGN FILMS

With the OO LA LA's and the LA DI DA's, she was mesmerized
By the movements and sounds of the far away places.
Although she could not completely understand, she loved to
watch her Foreign films.
She escaped herself into the cells, in black and white, and
in color...
On mountains, under towers, in castles and prisons,
Being rescued by her lover in waiting...

What would his name be today? Jacque? Pascal? Sven? Roberto?

Weekly visits to her local library did not out-number
Her nightly visitors in her unending dreams.
Low-lying clouds surrounded her bed, as she tucked herself in,
Flat on her back, waiting for sleep to find her...again.

What was she hoping for? What was she expecting?
Her life was dull, with work, minimal friends, watering
plants and yoga.
Her escape was her salvation.
Or so she thought.

Deep in meditation, her nightly lover came to life, breathing
air into her Lungs and whisking her off to cold, damp and

dark places.
His very presence warmed her diminishing soul.
He breathed life into her and she became lost in his eyes.

Each dawn, she awoke, exhausted from her nightly adventures.
Work was cumbersome.
No one called. No one visited. Her plants were dying.
She maintained her pre-occupation with her fantasy.

Where was the reality? Where was the trace of
human existence?

She was tired of becoming lost. She yearned to be validated,
But could not escape the confines of the prison
Of her own mind and cell.
Night came and the film had not reached its end.
Her eyes became heavy, while sitting on her divan.
One last adventure, she whispered to herself, as she
fell asleep.

While in between her reality and fantasy,
Her lover sat next to her draped body.
He held her body tight and kissed her passionately.
Her body rose, and her lungs filled with something foreign.
He breathed poison into her.
She remained his lover...forever.

MEN ARE SIMPLE: THE FOUR "S's": SLEEP, SPORTS, SEX AND SUSTENANCE

Women have it hard. Men have it easy.

From the time females are born, the majority of that time
is spent
Being motherly.
Nurturing.
Peacemakers.
People who take the time to tidy up after others.

Men are simple. Women are hard.
Why wouldn't we be? We become tired of taking care
of others
And we are last in line.
I haven't had a hot meal since 1982.

Men are simple. They require four things.
Sleep. Sports. Sex. Sustenance.
Women and men provide for the household, financially.
Women lack sleep. We are thinking of all the stuff that we
have to do Tomorrow.

When men sleep, they SLEEP.
They snore...

I haven't slept since 1982.
Women go shopping for all kinds of FOODS for the
SPORTING events.
Men dive wholeheartedly into their sporting events.
Eating. Drinking. Spilling.
Yelling for refills...
After the sporting events, they fall asleep, and then they have
SEX in the morning.

Women clean up, after sporting events.

Men are simple. They require only four things.

CRYING UNDER THE INFLUENCE

Fifty is the new black.

Time has gotten away from her and now it was her turn to have some fun.

How does one have fun, after fifty, when one has been the responsible one?

If managing a family, paying bills on time and being in bed at a decent hour Was an Olympic event, she would have the Gold.

But, as she approached fifty, her responsibilities were now just herself.

The irresponsible mate had cheated and left.

The little birds were no longer little.

They left the nest and made little birds of their own.

Giving dancing a try, she went with friends to night clubs.

She discovered that she could in fact dance,

So she danced for the rest of her life.

Giving skydiving a try, she went with chums to the air field.

She discovered that she loved to fly,

So she flew for the rest of her life.

Giving karaoke a try, she frequented her local bars on Tuesdays and Wednesdays.

She discovered that she could sing,

So she sang for the rest of her life.

In the mixture and the midst, spirits were a factor.
She did not need it, but the peer pressure was high.
Not knowing that saying No was a possibility, she partook
in the spirits
And discovered that all the spirits did for her,
Was produce uncontrollable tears.
Her current and past woes crept in her brain
And sobbing commenced to her dismay.

With pen to paper, she jotted down one future adventure
after another.
She worked. She dressed up. She put on makeup.
Pub crawls. Spirits. Crying under the influence. Festivals
and spirits. More crying...Car shows. Spirits. Crying under
the influence. Concerts. Oktoberfests. Fashion shows.
Sporting events. Outdoor Arenas.
And...the dreaded blind dates.

Spirits, spirits, spirits.

By the time she reached fifty-one, she was done.
Given the option of saying No, she said No,
And discovered that she was good at it.
She continued on with her adventures with friends,
Minus the spirits.
And she never cried again.

THE LIFE CYCLE OF THE HERMIT CRAB

She lived all her life undiagnosed.
On the surface she had it all together,
But in and around the depths of her psyche,
She was always yelling at herself to stop thinking.

Friends loved her, until they didn't.
Lovers loved her, until they didn't.
Family loved her, until they didn't.

Bound by a Christian upbringing, she was always polite
and kind.
Always helpful and giving.
Always mildly outspoken.
Always fun and funny.

On the surface she had it all together...

Friends loved her and were polite to her, until they weren't.
Lovers loved her and were accepting of her help and giving,
Until they weren't.
Family loved her and enjoyed her laughter, until they couldn't.

Isolation was her only solace,
Until the isolation metamorphosed her into a crab.

The crab would surface at work, at intended play,
At gatherings with friends, night and day.
Isolation was her only solace,
Until the isolation changed her into a hermit.
The hermit sat and sat until its heart began to harden.

She could not move from the confines of her room.
Is my life over? she asked aloud, to no one listening.
Her isolation was her undoing and in fact, her life was over.

She continued to die from within.
Her vessels hardened, her arteries hardened.
Her blood slowed and became thick.
Her skin hardened and she became immovable.

This is the life and death cycle of the hermit crab.

LIFE: A SLICE, A SLIVER, A SLAB OR A SMIDGEN

We are a product of our upbringing.
Are our lives predetermined by nature or nurture,
Or by fate or faith?
Is your current disposition a sum of all your experiences,
Good, bad or indifferent?

Life is meant to be lived, cherished, enjoyed and expanded.
Sharing is of the utmost importance, so share away...
Life is hard. Life is easy.
Life is too short...and the days are numbered.
Life is meant for community, companionship
And being in the service of others.

Grab the bull by the horns and run.
Grab the brass ring and fly.
Grab the liar and the cheaters and throw them to the wolves.

Rid yourself of pain and heartache, find your bliss and stick
with it.
Harm no one.
Ask for help. Go to church.
Join a group. Take a hike, and enjoy the creation of God.

Your life is not lived, if you take only a sliver or a smidgen,
You miss out on many things.
Be afraid, be cautious, but approach anyway.
You may get hurt, but is it not truly worth the risk?
You gain strength, where you thought you had none.

Take more than a smidgen, take a slice.
Don't take a sliver.

Take a slab of life, make it overflowing doses of
adventure, fun,
Honesty and truth.
Don't be fooled.
Don't be taken advantage of.
Know your enemies and stay away.
Rid yourself of those who are toxic.
Never give second chances.

Rid yourself of pain and heartache, find your bliss and stick
with it.
Life is meant to be lived, cherished, enjoyed and expanded.
Share what you know,
Let the love in...
And live life, by the slab.

I WANT TO BE A PICTURE FRAME MODEL

I want to be a picture frame model,
Where everyone would see me every day...
You walk by me, ponder me, see me and say, that I
look familiar.
Where do I know that girl?

I want to be a picture frame model,
To go to your home and see what I am missing...
I could sit on your mantel, be frozen in a mesmerizing smile.
What are you thinking, girl?

Pick me up, dust me off, pretend that I am your lover.
Pick me up, dust me off and say Goodnight to me,
every night...
Put me back in my place or move me around,
Touch me gently with your fingertips,
Just say Goodbye to me daily, as you walk out that door.

I want to be a picture frame model,
Who comes to life after you go to bed.
I will walk out from my 8 by 10 frame, slither down
your furniture
And stretch to be true.
What is your next move, girl?

I will climb your stairs, saunter down the hall,
Quietly open your door and wonder.
Hush, girl, he is sleeping.
Hush girl, she is sleeping.
Hush girl, they are sleeping.

I will forever keep watch, whispering in your ear,
Smiling back at you, when you smile at me.
Decorate my frame,
Hold me tight,
I will not leave you.

Move me around into another frame, have me face the wall,
When you have some shame.
I swear she is staring at me!
I am.

I want to be a picture frame model,
Frozen in smile, frozen in time, forever in your thoughts,
Forever a part of you.

...LATELY, SOMETIMES...

...lately, I cannot sleep. But, I am exhausted.
I over-eat, I under-eat, I over-think...
...sometimes, I forget.

...lately, I weep uncontrollably, I feel numb, I feel lonely, I am
somewhere between Robin's egg and Periwinkle...
...sometimes, Azure.

...lately, I cannot stop my thinking of you.
You show up UN-announced, UN-accepted, UN-wanted...
...sometimes, I wonder if you think about me.

...lately, I hear whispering in my ear, but you are not there...
I jump at the thought of you, I curse at myself for not being able
to stop the thinking of you...
What is this power that I cannot control?
...sometimes, I dwell.

...lately, I get excited, confused, wishing, praying...
I have wondered why you could not be more tolerant of my
uniqueness,
of just me...
Why were you not stronger than I?
...sometimes, I dismiss.

...lately, I face the reality of the ending of it all, the end is coming soon, by choice or by chance...and I welcome the inevitable darkness...

...lately, the darkness
...sometimes, the light.

...lately, I no longer risk my heart, my mind, my body, my soul...
I no longer wish to be needed and I seek out the darkness to surround me, enveloping my entire physical being and I long for true and solid sleep...

But...
...lately, as I have laid in the darkness, the whispering comes to me, welcomed...and calls me by name and tells me that life is for loving, taking risks, opening up despite the possibility of pain, sorrow, rejection, confusion...sometimes...

And...
...lately, I am believing that I am worthy, having some ounce of faith, that wasn't there before...having faith in myself and in the world around me...

...still apprehensive, but hopeful, feeling blessed...
...lately...and sometimes.

SIMPLY COMPLICATED

Are you empathetic, tolerant, understanding?
For I am simply complicated.

You are too, and I know it, but you are unable to recognize
and admit it...

I cry, but you will never see...
I laugh, and you can see...
...that I am simply complicated.

I get mad and you will not see,
I am happy and that you have seen...
I'm simply complicated.

We react. I let you know. I say so...
And sometimes you just know...

When I don't feel well, I ache.
Not so complicated.

I think...
Simply complicated.
I worry.
Simply complicated.

I am.
Not so complicated.

I breath. I am. I love. I create.
Not so complicated.

But...

I need.
I want...
To not be so simply complicated.

REMEMBER ME

Remember me.
Remember me, not for the things that I own,
But for the things that I have done.

...not for the things that I have said,
But for the things that I did not mean to...
...for the things that I said that made you feel appreciated...

Remember me for the beautiful things that I have created...
I have created with His help, His instruction,
His understanding, and His love...

Remember me for my laughter, my sense of humor, my
sparkle in my eyes When I smile at every moment that I
see you.

Remember me for my ability to listen, to enjoy, for my
understanding,
My thirst, my empathy...
...of your day, your needs, your wishes and desires...

Remember me for my dancing, cartwheels, excitement
and love...
Of everything.

For as I continue in my state of energy, these are the things that I will Remember YOU for,
These are the things that will carry me into the next heart-beat,
The next moment, the next blink, the next flutter.

Remember me for the wholeness of me...
For I will always remember you.

WHAT'S A GIRL TO DO?

There's always someone prettier.
There is always someone taller.
There is always someone skinnier.

What's a girl to do?

There's always someone more educated.
There is always someone more organized.
There is always someone with a perfect family,
Better than mine.
Not to mention, more money.

What's a girl to do?

We are all deserving...of love, peace and contentment,
So why am I a Troll magnet?
It is beyond my current understanding.

I want to be loved, cherished and understood, not just
Tolerated, laughed at and called for, at your convenience.

All I needed from you...was to be stronger.
All I want from you...is to walk away forever and leave me
in pieces...

Until I can put myself back together...

I want to drift away, but your smell, taste...addicting smile
And abundant charm,
Has me obsessive,
Quite possessive,
And in an unending state of confusion.

For I have given you all that I possess. All that I am.
All of my heart, mind, body and soul...and I have nothing left
to give...
I have nothing left to offer...

So, what's a girl to do?

Find my strength from within, to be the bigger person,
walk away,
Facing many tears, many sleepless nights,
And the sounds of my own wailing echoing in my own ears.

I know that with all of what's left of my heart, that ultimately
I will be fine.
And one day...love will find me, when I least expect it,
For I will not be looking again.

I pray that love will find me...before my broken heart's last beat...

...so THAT is what this girl will do...

CAPABLE

I am NOT capable, even with all the words available,
To express my feelings for you.

I love your voice, your smile, your laugh,
Your arms, shoulders...your touch.

I urge for the chills to continue up my spine,
Into my heart and to resonate throughout me.
I get more than excited to hear from you, to learn from you,
To experience all that I can with you...

I want to learn all that my body can do, all that my soul
can do,
All that my heart can endure...

Of that, I am capable...

Waves of excitement, waves of bliss gush from me,
To you, into you, around you...
Waves of dizziness, light-headedness...
Sparkles of light, blinding, external, internal,
eternal celebration...

Warmth, closeness, safety, longing, pressure and release,

Wanting, hoping, melting, tension, repeating, breathing,
Ebbs and floes, holding my breath...

Of that, I am capable...

YOUR SUIT

Your DAY suit is blue, tan and yellow...
...stiff, professional, right, determined...

Your NIGHT suit is white, green, brown...
...easy, excited, loose, free, uninhibited, earthy...

Your DAY suit is responsible, powerful, red, shyly playful,
laughing, nourishing, even sometimes apprehensive
and guarded...

Your NIGHT suit is passionately purple, giving, wanting,
pushing, pulling, stroking...
Sometimes your suit shows up as armor...

Your NIGHT suit is pink, smiling, relaxed, free, spiritual, safe
and yearning...

Unable to wear your suit, night and day, you wear it when
you can,
When you want...
When you have to...

I awake, wondering which suit will you be wearing this day...
Which suit shall I wear, that suits you?

AS IS

It has taken me more time than I wanted,
As I enter this next chapter,
To finally accept myself...

As is.

I can do, what I can accomplish.
I am hopeful and afraid, at the same time, of what is left of
my life.

I own things, but it is not what I need to get by...
I surround myself with color, pictures, paint, tapestries,
Light, candles, music, food.
Sights and smells that...trigger happy and sad memories of
my life.

I am afraid for how much I can love, for fear of losing it, for
fear of it all
Going away again, of all of it disappearing into the vastness...
And no one knowing.
...no one even noticing when I disappear...

I accept my fear, as is...

Can I get by without expression, without communication?
Will I get hurt...again?
Will I survive it?
Just how much can I truly endure?...
Just how much am I capable of risking...again?
Why won't this pain just kill me?

I accept all of my questions, as is...

I love myself.
I rely on myself and no other...
It has been a long struggle, but I do...
It is a lonely address...

I love life.
I love my children...
I am blessed with all that is necessary...that surrounds me.

As long as I live, I love.
As is...

BEING

Tingling.

Anticipation, desire, love, lust...
The need to be touched, to be loved, wanted and needed,
Cherished and desired...

What is waiting for me each day, I do not know.

I must raise up my head, my hands and give thanks for
waking, for being...
For another day of sunshine, light and blue skies,...
Clouds and flowers...the songs of birds,
The playful singing of children across the way...

What waits for me each day, each heart beat, each blink of
my eyes?

I look at you and wonder, what are you wondering, too?

Do you look forward to seeing me, being with me?
Do you look forward to touching me, as much as I want
To be touched by you?
Are you thankful for me,
For meeting me,

For being with me?

Are you thankful for being?

ACCEPT ME

Accept me for who I am,
For my quirkiness, my oddness, my silliness.
For I accept you.

When you accept, you are alive, you are free.

Accept me for my smile, my laughter, my humor.
For I accept that of you.

Accept me for my sadness,
For I cry at times, at the drop of a hat...
Any hat, any size, any color, any style...

Accept me for my height, my weight, my face, my size, my
eye color,
My hair color, even as it is turning grey...reminding me of
my numbered days.

...for my skin tone, my choice of clothing, even if to you
It may not match or be what you would wear...
Despite what others may say, polka dots and stripes DO
go together.

When you accept, you are alive, you are free.

Accept me for accepting you, for I will not judge you or even hate you.

Accept me for my kindness to you, my
politeness, courteousness,
And do not forget to thank my parents for all of that...

Accept me for welcoming you into my life, for I welcome you unconditionally.
Accept me for accepting you, for you are kind, kind-hearted, sweet, lovely, beautiful, for accepting me.

I CANNOT AFFORD

I cannot afford for you to be my friend.
You are toxic and mean and selfish.
You have proven that you do not truly care for me...

I cannot afford for you to be my lover.
For you are a liar, a cheater and you steal.
You exposed me to the possibilities of diseases and harm.

I cannot afford to have a conversation with you.
You yell, you cuss and take the Lord's name in vain.
You say terrible things about people that you don't
even know.

I cannot afford to meet you for lunch, coffee or tea.
You lie, you gossip, you exaggerate, you are not funny.
You embarrass me and belittle me in public.
Stop trying so hard...to be what you are not...

I cannot afford to take a walk with you.
If I was in front of you, I would not be sure
That you would not push me down.
I will not go near a cliff with you.

I cannot afford to work with you.

You would stab me in the back to climb up that ladder.
I'd rather that you stab me in the front.
I don't need that ladder as much as you think you deserve it.
You are not entitled to anything.
Not even the air that you breathe.

I cannot afford to trust you.
You have proven time and time again, that you cannot
be trusted,
Because you lie, cheat and steal.
I cannot afford to allow you to do that to me again.

I cannot afford to trust myself, for time and time again,
You were my friend, my lover.
We had great conversations, we took walks,
I worked with you, side by side,
And you stole my heart.
You cheated on me and you lied.

I cannot afford to trust myself,
For if I got near you, I would want to talk to you,
Work with you,
Touch you,
And walk with you.
And I would push you over that cliff...

LIVE MEMORIAL SERVICE

Why wait until I die, for you to tell me how you feel?
Why wait until I die, to say what you really wanted to say?

Have my memorial service today, now, in front of me,
With friends and family gathering around, telling stories about me,
To me.

Tell me that you had fun with me, with many
great conversations.
Tell me that you missed me, every time that I went away.
Tell me that you were entertained, with every joke I told.
Tell me that I am beautiful, here and now.

Why wait until I die to fall in love with me?
Why wait until I die to tell me that you love me?

Have my memorial service today, here and now,
And sincerely express that you will always love me,
Love everything about me,
And never let me go.

Express to me what you like about me,
My unique freckled face,

Janean Phillips

My unending and enchanting smile,
My animated and outrageous stories,
My children, my family, my friends,
My curiosity and adventure for life.

Tell me that you loved all the notes that I left for you.
Tell me that you looked forward to seeing me, hearing how
my day was...
Tell me that you don't mind that I talk a lot.
Tell me that you love the way my mind works.
Tell me that you want to live the rest of your life with me.

I am here, so why wait?
I am one phone call away, so why wait?
I am one message away, so why wait?

Why wait until I die, to tell me how you feel?

CHAPTERS IN LIFE

In the first chapter of my life, I was introduced to the world.
Willing, able and ready to face the world, and all it had to offer.
I was a sponge, a magnet, a willing participant to learn, see
and do.
I was fed, clothed, housed and taken care of...
I was a child, and children grow up...

In the next chapter of my life, I was alive and noticed.
Full of energy, sports, opinions and puppy love.
I was a sponge, a cootie, not always a willing participant to
listen, see and do.
I was fed, clothed, housed and disciplined.
I was a teenager, and children grow up...

In the next few decades, I got married and had children,
I went to school and lost friends.
And I lost my identity.
I fed, I clothed, I housed and I disciplined.
I argued. I bought. I sold. I yearned. I craved. I sought. I met...

Before the next chapter, my family was destroyed by
cheating and lies.
My children were willing participants to listen, learn, see
and do.

We escaped.
We argued. We ate. We bought. We yearned. We worked.
We were alive...

In that next chapter, my children grew up.
They learned. They met. They craved. They loved.
I said Goodbye.
College. Marriage. Work. Children of their own.

In the proceeding chapters, I was full of energy, hope, wonder and worry.
I loved. I lived. I sought out numerous adventures.
I kept trustworthy friends.
I sought out new friends.
I argued. I worked. I cried. I met. I fell in love.
I was destroyed...again.
And again. And again.

In the last chapter of my life, I was full of faith.
Willing, able and ready to face death from this world and all it had to offer.
I was a sponge, a magnet,
And a willing participant to listen, learn, see and do.

I was fed. I was clothed. I was housed. I was taken care of,
I was loved, I was a child...and I grew up.

TWO HITS OUT ON JASMINE

She did nothing wrong. She was just born.
She was beautiful from day one.
Perfect in every way, shape and her form.
Her hair was rust red, her skin was creamy white.
Her eyes were wonderfully green.

Her family loved her. Her family blessed her.
She was a perfect addition to their lives.

Girls hated her. Boys hated her.

She had it all. A good home.
A great heart. A voice given to her by angels.
A mind as sharp as tacks and a tongue that made people melt.

Women hated her. Men hated her.

She did nothing wrong. She was just born.
Women plotted, were jealous, and gossiped about her.
Men admired her, idolized her, were unholy in their thoughts
about her...

She had it all. A perfect sense of humor.
A college education. A wonderful, saintly man by her side.

Janean Phillips

She did nothing wrong. She was just born.

Jasmine was sweet, kind, giving and creative.
She used her influence for good, while evil was working
against her.
She had many acquaintances, whom she thought were
her friends.
One covetous man, one green woman, who sought out
to destroy
This wonderful creation.

With weapon in hand and in mind, one meeting later,
There were two hits out on Jasmine.
Unknowing, oblivious and living with faith, she walked home,
Like every other day.

In one single moment, her sense of humor was destroyed.
In one single moment, her voice was taken from her.
In one single moment, her red hair turned white, her white
skin turned red.

Her great heart continued to pump.
Her beautiful green eyes continued to see.
Her mind continued to think and her tongue made
everyone melt.

She did nothing wrong. She was just born.
Her family loved her. Her family blessed her.
She was a perfect addition to her new family.

ALTERNATE LANDINGS

Fifty-one freckles and fifty-one years of age,
All dressed up and no where to go.
This was her boring life.
This was her alternate life.

Sleep was over, she landed on her feet, yoga was done,
The radio was on and getting ready for work commenced.
Packing a snack, singing along to the music with no
other audience
Than that of her irritated neighbors.

Beige pants, blue shirt, plain 'ole shoes, grey bandana.
Work was work, the wage was shameful and saving
was difficult.
Work was over and going home commenced.
How she got home, she did not know.

Her mind would wander, her hopes got high.
She dreamed herself being better off, full of life and love
and happiness.
She dreamed herself in a ample home,
A different beautiful dress every night.
She dreamed of wearing high heels, colorful handbags,
Earrings and necklaces that matched, painted fingernails

And perfect hairstyles.

Dodging cars and traffic lights, she dreaded going home to her humble life.
It was too quiet. It was too cold.
It was empty of a love of which she longed.
The same old pasta, the same old water, the same old shows,
Comfy pajamas and wooly socks, a landed place on her couch.
The television droned, while she worked very hard to keep her eyes open.

In her dreams, her alternate life flourished.
She visited lands afar, her faceless lover was always near, always sincere.
She felt loved and cherished, she was told that she was beautiful
And she believed.
Her arms felt full, the spirits of her children lived in her heart.
The grass was deep green, the sky was piercing blue.
She landed on a swing with her lover.

Sleep was over, she landed on her feet.
Yoga was done. Her shower was over.
She dressed in beige, blue, black and grey.
The radio was on. She sang to no one listening.
How she got to work, she did not know.

COLLECTING MISTAKES, WITH A COLLECTOR

"Must be nice living in that bubble," her son said,
As he packed for his second year in college.
Her retort was off the cuff, as she commented that it was safe.
Go meet, he said, go live, he said, go love, he said, and have some fun.
So adhering to the advice, she did.

One by one, she did just that. She met new friends, young and old,
And coworkers, young and old,
She lived and had fun, with bikes and hikes, trails and rails,
Sports of water, land and air, dancing into the night at concerts and clubs.
She got burned, she peeled, she was exhausted and loved it.
She met one collector after another, who
temporarily un-walled
Their narrow minds and narrow hearts to reel her in...

I find you intriguing, they would say.
And as time passed, she began to despise it.
Why did they all say that?
That was the constant clue she chose to ignore.
What is intriguing all about? she would ask.

Aha, a Collector, who gathers acquaintances, uses hearts and breaks them,
And has never had one true friend.

They came to her doorstep by the dozens,
And she learned over time, to ignore them all.
The ones who broke her heart were long gone,
But they truly lingered in her thoughts.

In her dreams, she would play out the meetings of the few collectors
With whom she allowed to come in.
She cried while drifting. She cried while waking.
That became a feat to defeat.
What is this intriguing all about? she would cry.
I am just me, adventurous and giddy, deserving to be treated in kind.

I accept Pirates, Wenches, Gypsies and Travelers.
Collectors are Vultures, they are Vampires, they are Vermin.
They are Collectors.

I need no more Collectors in my life.
Do not ignore the clues, girl: No friends, no close coworkers,
No relationships with their mothers, no dads to speak of...

Bars and homes were the limits of their recreational existence.
Vile comments in clusters, here and there,
Meant to be humorous, but cannot be ignored.
Despite her love, she eventually learned to run,
The moment that it was voiced.
She learned to recognize the Collectors and high tail it
To the safety of her dim-lit home.

Her hair was raised. Shivers ran down her spine.
Alone is good, she would say.
Dim is good, she would say.
Pleasant thoughts, open minds and compassionate hearts
Are what she needed to surround herself to live free.

She no longer collected her greatest mistakes.
She no longer gravitated toward Collectors.

BEING COMFORTABLE IN ONE'S OWN SKIN

Could it be?
Children can be cruel, taking notice of differences
and verbalizing
To the point of embarrassment and harassment and bullying...
We are a product of our parents.
Those children grow up to be adults, physically,
But everyone knows that they never grow up...

My hair is different than yours.
My height is different from yours.
My face is definitely different from yours.
My upbringing is surely different from yours.
So what?

Some try to shoot down my confidence, but I will never let
them see it wane,
For it has waned from time to time, given my choices of friends,
Current and past...
Comfortable people, like me, DO make mistakes...

I am told that I am intimidating.
NO! I am comfortable in my own skin.
I am told that I have a "kick ass, ask questions later" attitude.

Janean Phillips

NO! I am comfortable in my own skin.
I am told that I am boastful.
NO! I am proud and comfortable...
We are a product of our own parents.

I am told that I should not dance on bars,
That no one cares that I walk into a room as if I own it,
That I should not do cartwheels or get excited about anything,
That I should not accept everyone and anyone...
That I should be more selective with whom I choose to love.,
That no one cares that I am youthful looking in this
next chapter...

Why wouldn't I be? I pray that I can continue to throw
My woes and worries to the wind,
Having faith that all will come out rainbows in the end.
When I kick you to the curb, my wrinkles subside.
NO! I am comfortable and it is I who does not care, about you.

I kick you to the curb!

I am comfortable in my own skin.
Why aren't you?

SNOWBALL

It's a snowball's chance in hell that I would see you here today.
And yet, here you are!
I dreaded this moment, for moments on end,
And yet, I lived through it.
My gut spoke to me, my heart spoke to me, my soul spoke to me
And told me that you would be present.
Although you should not be...

You are a painful reminder of all of my mistakes,
You represent a massive, irreversible rejection and heartache
That remains an open wound for all to see.

You have no rights to me, no rights to be near me, no rights
to even speak.
You have no rights, yet here you are.
Looking as beautiful as the last time I saw you.
How dare you?

Congratulations! Since your goal was to hurt my feelings,
you succeeded!
I am a shell of a human being, because of your betrayal.
I am a shell of a human being, just getting by, day to day,
Because of your lies.
I am a shell of a human being, with a damaged heart,

Because of your cheating.

The winter sets in and makes my heart ungenerous.
I hate the snow...
The spring returns and whereas I should be filled with hope
and promise, I am filled with dread and doom.
Summer rears its hot head and still my heart is cold.
The fall comes around and it happens all over again.
The snowball rolls down this incessant hill, gathering more
snow and growing.

Is she sitting in my chair at your table?
Does she love you, like I loved you?
Will she embrace your children, like I did once?

When will my reprieve come to me?
When the polar winds have finally subsided, when summer
starts to cool,
Or when the leaves begin to turn, when the rains come in
the spring?

The snowball will continue to roll down this hill, growing
and growing,
Until it reaches Hades in the end, evaporating...and starting
all over again
As rain...

LETTING GO

I thought that I could continue on this path, this
wonderful adventure.
But I realize I cannot, I realize that somehow
I want more of you than you are willing to give.
It makes me sad that I'd rather leave and have nothing,
Than to stay and accept the situation as is...

But I want to be a part of your life, more than an
occasional friend...
I am sorry that you believe that I am not good enough for you.
Perhaps it is the other way around.
I want to be a part of someone's family, but it is an agenda that
I am not able to push.
I don't know why I can't be more like a guy!
For guys seem to enjoy the status quo.
Women fall so easily, for we inherently bond within
An instance of a meeting...

Thank you for being a part of my life, despite it being so brief.
I wonder if it is true, what they say, that one cannot truly be
in love,
If it is not reciprocated.
If so, I have never really been loved.
I am trying to categorize all these emotions of confusion, love,

Fear, hatred, hope, envy, worthiness...
Being involved with men certainly has lowered my IQ.
I cannot afford to lose more brain cells.

I have come to realize that I comply out of a sense of feeling quite lost.
It has been my foolish notion of hope that keeps me going.
This time with you, has been different than the others.
So therefore, it is that one thing that has reassured me to stop looking...
Until now.

You are the most interesting man in the world, that I have met so far.
However, the world is vast and so is my imagination.
Just like you, I am trying to find my place in this life...
And so far, I have placed myself into strange predicaments.
Until now.

My crying comes from knowing that I will miss you.
I have come to love your company and stories and watching your face.
I can still feel your arms wrapped around me.
My crying comes from knowing that you do love me,
But not in the way that I need you to...
I deserve better, and better is what you are unable to provide.

At Whitt's End

Your lifestyle is foreign to me.
I need to fall out of love with you.
But it is hard to give up this feeling of euphoria,
When euphoria is all that one seeks.
I have danced in my heart.
But I must hang up my dancing shoes.

As I am bound to isolate myself to cure myself of this disease
called love,
I fear that I will shut down and disappear.
I promise myself to never buy a cat or a rocking chair.

Am I doomed to never love again and doomed to never find
my bliss?
Only time will tell as I watch the hourglass of letting go...

BLIND DATE NUMBER ONE: YOU ARE NOT FUNNY

We spoke on the phone before we met,
I should have known better, to have ended it there.
You asked me why I have not dated in over six years,
As if to ask, "Just how ugly are you?"
I told you that I was busy, with three jobs and
raising children,
But still I am sure you wondered.
So, with slight hesitation, I agreed to meet you...
A mistake that I wish I could have taken back.

Only meeting you through others I made an assumption
That meeting at your home was a good idea.
How wrong must I continue to be?
I picked up a pizza and drove for miles, excited and concerned.
You opened the door, and damn you were the one who
was ugly.

But given my naïve upbringing, I give everyone a chance
And you were included in that ludicrous mindset.
We ascended the stairs in your overly clean apartment.
We briefly retired to the couch for idle chitchat.
We briefly sat in the kitchen and ate, as you silently slid a
coaster my way.

You jokingly said that you should call your mother,
For when you told your mother I was meeting you,
She called me a hussy...
"Call your mother," I said, "for the elderly do not scare me"...
I should have left then...
How wrong must I continue to be?
You asked if I was done eating, when all I had consumed was
Three pieces of squared little pizza.

I was done, but not with the pizza.

We retired to the couch, where your big screen TV was on.
Keith Urban was singing and gyrating, so I could
not concentrate
On what you were saying.
It was more like droning anyway, for you told me
What you had been doing since 1981.
By 9:30 I did not receive my rescue phone call.
By 9:31 I was ready to leave.
You told me that I could stay, for I needed not to feel an urge
to leave,
Although you had to get up at 430am to work.
You expected me to stay, since I came to your home,
So perhaps your mother was right?
In reality, I was wrong to have come over, but curiosity got
the best of me.

You mentioned again, that I need not leave, citing that you
had some rope.
"Not funny," I said, as I grabbed the leftover pizza
And headed for the door.
You slammed your back again the double doors at
the entryway,
Stating, "Do not open these doors, for that is where I hide
The dead bodies."
"Funny!" I said, grabbing doorknob in hand...
As I rushed to my car, readying my keys and readying my
screaming voice.

The door flew open, I threw my pizza and handbag inside
And quickly sat my ass down in the drivers seat.
You stood there, holding the door, asking if you could call me
By another name.
"No! that is not my name," I sternly replied.

Without no other good words that I could think of saying,
I thanked you for having me over.
I stated that we should be honest,
So I told you that I did not find you attractive,
And that that would be the last time we would ever speak.

You accepted my insult with grace and humility, but I
knew better.

You did not agree with me and I am sure you recovered quickly.
Rest assured that I had only a few nightmares for only a
few days.

Besides the rope and dead bodies, your face was the
ultimate nightmare.

I lived through my first Blind Date,
I told myself Never Again!!
How wrong must I continue to be?

BLIND DATE NUMBER TWO: WHEN WILL I EVER LEARN?

I am convinced that my girlfriends do not like me,
For trolls are all with whom they have set me up.
We spoke on the phone before we met.
And as always, I thought, This one sounds nice.

When will I ever learn?

You described yourself as being somewhere between
Shaggy and Norris.
I described myself as looking like a grandmotherly,
Short librarian.

We agreed to meet at a restaurant, so as usual, I got
there early.
Dressed to the nines, I was feeling quite chipper.
You walked in and headed straight for the bar.
Already, I did not like you.
You are a liar.
There is no Chuck in that man!
I told myself...

I motioned to you and you came right over.
Beer in one hand and a wine glass in the other,

You plopped right down and the droning began.
Your dad dropped you off and you already ate dinner?
So what are we meeting for?

You told me to order and that you would treat.
Damn skippy, I told myself, so that is what I did.
I mentioned your piercing blue eyes
And you complimented my dazzling smile.

When my pasta arrived, I ate some with a fork,
While you picked at mine with unclean and unkempt
Fingernails. Really?

You told me that you brought a camera,
And after dinner, you'd like to take pictures of me,
In the grass, in the park across the street.
Hell, no.
Your only good quality were your eyes,
And the fact that your heart would stop beating...some day.

When will I ever learn?

Because your dad had dropped you off,
I felt as if I had to take you home.
So, before we did that, I agreed to drive you to
A pit stop on the way, so that is what I did.

Over a beer, an argument ensued between you and
your friend.
Money was what was owed,
And high-tailing it was what I did.
Get your ass in the car now! Was what I told you,
As I put the car in Drive.
You jumped in and away we went.
Silence was what I needed and you complied.

When will I ever learn!

Once at your parent's house, we entered inside.
Your parents were adorable!
You must have been adopted.
You disappeared, while I sat on the couch
And conversed with your father.
Your mother wore a duster and sat nearby.

"You're not like all the other girls that my son has dated,"
Your father stated.
"You talk in complete sentences!"
"You have all of your teeth!
And a pretty smile, too."
"Oh my goodness, you are also employed?"
"She's a keeper," your mother added.

I now believe in Hell.
I made a note to myself to immediately find a church.

When will I ever learn?

You walked me to my car and requested a kiss.
Hell no, I thought, but stated just a No.
I had only one opportunity to not mince words,
So I told you that I thought you had a drinking problem,
That I did not find you attractive...and as I screeched out
Of the driveway, I told you to Take Care.

I am convinced that my girlfriends hate me.
When will I ever learn?

BLIND DATE NUMBER THREE:
YOU HAVE GOT TO BE JOKING!

Why can't I meet a man, not in a bar?
For barflies, I do not need.
I knew his sister, so I thought he would be safe.
But how safe can barflies be?

We agreed to meet at a pizza joint.
Regardless, I put on my best dress and high heels,
High hair and a big smile.
He showed up in black dingy jeans, a cut-off T,
Dulled cowboy boots and hairy armpits.

You have got to be joking!

Since he could not make an effort, why should I?
Regardless, I was personable and listened intently.
Plus I was hungry...
As we ate dinner, I was amazed of all of the foul
That had come out of his mouth.

My mind began to wander, as he cussed and
Insulted every age bracket, nationality, heritage
And group, that his narrow mind could come up with...
I wondered what I looked like to him,

AT WHITT'S END

As he may have thought that I was one to
Put up with such nonsense, such narrow-mindedness.

I stopped sipping in my straw, midstream
When he made the comment about hanging
People of color in the hallways at school back in 1977.
I guessed that it would not have been a good time
To tell him about my children...

You have got to be joking!

Were these outrageous stories suppose to impress me
Or be insulting to me? I was the latter...
His final blow was the suggestion that we get together
With an additional girl, to pounce and pound,
I informed him straight away, that I was formerly
Catholic, and I do not do such things.

You have got to be joking!
He exclaimed...

The conversation shifted, as he talked of his mother.
He began to cry, as he told me about her death.
He cried some more, as it was apparent that
He had regrets.
I touched his hand, reassuring him that she did

In fact love him and was proud of him.

He smiled and apologized for his ranting and
Embarrassing display of sadness and sorrow.
I suggested therapy, less alcohol, less foul language,
And less cologne.
I told him to take care of himself, that I was no longer
Interested in continuing the date.
He begged me to come over to his home and hang out.

You have got to be joking!

He stood up, cussed me out, as he called me everything
But a child of God.
He slammed down his fist on the table and left,
Continuing to call me names, that I was one hundred percent
Sure, that did not apply to me at all.

Briefly, it was an excitable moment.
I was thankful that he was gone.
The audience finally began to breathe and so did I.
My eyes lowered. The pizza still looked inviting,
Despite the recent drama.

One by one, the other patrons came over.
They scooted their tables and chairs towards me,

Inviting me to become a part of their party,
And so I did.

We ate. We drank.
I told them what was said,
And we laughed until we cried.

And I was not joking...

BLIND DATE NUMBER FOUR: TWENTY MINUTES

My efforts were for naught, with a perfect coiffure and manicured nails.
The date was set up, days in advance, but for whatever excuses,
He was running late.

I occupied myself with mindless television, for at least an hour.
He called, apologized and asked to meet an hour later.
I wasn't busy, so why not?

I ran an errand, for snacks and wine,
But as I got home, he called, apologized and asked for another hour.
I commented that it would be quite ok
To meet on another day,
But he promised that it wouldn't be much longer.

So, I went to the pool hall and played a round.
Ate some chips and had a beer,
Chit-chatted with friends and flirted with some patrons,
As I waited...

He called again, and was ready to meet,
So I high-tailed it to the restaurant.

At Whitt's End

I ordered an appetizer, water and a beverage,
When he walked on in.

He smiled, plopped across from me, then turned his body.
He sat in the booth, with legs propped in the bench,
Turned his baseball cap around and slammed his back
Against the partition.

Just like that, with all his time wasted and mine,
The date was over in less than twenty minutes.
His body language spoke volumes,
As if to say, "You are not my kinda girl."

What was he looking for?
With his imperfect body, beer belly, short stature
And disheveled clothing?

You are right, sir, I am not your kinda girl.

I had fun shopping for much-needed alcohol,
And hiking up my skirt at the pool hall.
I was excited to have won the world record
For the world's shortest blind date.

MORE BLIND DATES

I am not perfect, this I know,
But I seek kindness, honesty, patience and fun.
He must be free from syndromes and drama,
Not cruel, not boastful, not so damn introverted.

If you don't have all of your teeth,
You need not apply.
If you have cheated on your wife,
You need not apply.
If you have lied to your girlfriend,
You need not apply.

"She's just crazy," they would say.
"She's a psycho."
"She's bi-polar."

Why wouldn't she be?
Women by nature, have such a wide range of emotions and
more emotions, than the two that you have...

"You have a beautiful smile."
"I was married three times."
"I have an addiction to... (...insert any word here...)"
"I find you intriguing."

"I knew you would judge me."

Who wouldn't?
But I wasn't, because I don't...but I am now.

"You should be thin by now.
You had your child twenty-three years ago."
Ouch. You just called me fat!
Should we talk about your chicken legs and pale skin?

"You are lacking six inches.
I am used to dating longer-legged women."
How would you like it if I told you that YOU were lacking
six inches?
As long as other parts of me are working,
What difference should that make?
I do have an active imagination and a curious brain.

"You would not be able to get a job as a Rep...of anything.
You know what I mean."
Do I ever.
In so many words, you just called me ugly!
Have you looked in the mirror lately?

"Your dress would look great on my floor."
Never gonna happen, dude.

"Please wear a black and red dress, so it will match my tie."
Why would I care about matching anything that you'd
be wearing?
"Have some wine. It will relax you."
I didn't start drinking until I turned forty, plus I'm driving.
So No.
"Catholics and Jews can marry, ya know?"
Yes, I am aware of that.
"Catholics and Mormons can marry, ya know?'
Yes, I knew that, too.
"How do you see us in a year?"
I don't see us...doing anything...past tonight!
"I think we should skip dessert here, and go have dessert at
my place."
I'm full...and home is where I am going.

Thanks, and No thanks.
I am not perfect, this I know.
You are not perfect, this I clearly know.
Thank you for showing your true colors and true thoughts.
When you start to walk on water, give me a call.
Or better yet, Don't.

If you are kind and honest and patient, and you don't have
any teeth,
Feel free to apply...

TIME OF YEAR

Fall is the best of all of the seasons.
It is my favorite time of year.
Halloween is my Christmas, with decorations and
costumes galore.
Days and days of people-watching, creative cooking and
seemingly endless
Invites to parties and staying up until sunrise.

The air is crisp, the sun sits perfectly in the sky, the wind
is curious.
Jeans, jackets, sweaters, boots and hats of all colors...
Like the fall, I am restless, but energetic,
I am thankful and thoughtful and I wonder...

Despite it being my favorite, I dread what comes after it.
Winter is a cruel, heartless bitch, and I need to slap her,
Before she kills me.
My sensitive Irish skin just cannot handle another cold spell.
I want to run away from home, to somewhere warm and sunny.
Anywhere tropical...

In addition to it being my favorite, fall is perfect for
making love.
One has to scramble to remove clothing, to duck under covers

And snuggle with a warm body.
...any warm body...
And warm up, with caresses and touches and deep
passionate kisses.

Fall is best, for when one is in love.
Holding firm hands, taking long walks or snuggling on
the couch,
With popcorn in one hand,
And the other hand over the eyes,
While torturing oneself with scary visions.
Holding tightly to a strong arm, while his hand is placed
Securely on my thigh.

I've enjoyed the sounds of the crinkling leaves, the
acorns dropping,
The different chirps of the birds who stayed behind.
One can crack open a window at night, and enjoy a
slight breeze.
Curling up in the sheets and down comforters.
Tiny bursts of welcomed shivers, as one awakens from
sound slumbers.

Hot chocolate warms the tummy.
Jogs at dawn, to get the heart pumping.
Welcome smiles from passersby.

At Whitt's End

And welcomed smiles from loved ones.
One can sit in the breakfast nook or by the fire,
Warming the toes and contemplating life.

I miss those days of welcoming smiles, of breakfast
nook sitting,
Of conversations of just any little 'ole thing.
As I watch my reflection get withered in the window,
The leaves are turning brown and falling like feathers to
the ground.
The laughter of the children is distant, for it seems.

I must be honest, for there are no more conversations.
I must be honest, for there are no more nights of breezes
of slight...
I must be honest, that hot chocolate warms the tummy,
But there are no more jogs at dawn, smiles from loved ones,
Nor nights of making love.

Fall is my favorite time of year.
But I dread for what comes after it.

NOTHING CAN DESCRIBE

Nothing can describe the feeling of holding a baby,
With tiny toes, a tiny nose and perfect baby's breath.
Nothing can describe being a witness to this life,
Watching this being grow and become a remarkable person.

When I first held my son, in my arms, as he rested on my chest,
Nothing can describe the feeling of overwhelming love
That I felt at that moment, and all the moments afterwards.
Watching him grow up and become a man, is quite wonderful.

He was like a sponge, absorbing all kinds of information
At record speed.
His eyes sparkled when he would see something,
Curious as a boy could be.
He sang with such perfect pitch, danced when I danced,
Played and learned, and grew to be decent and outstanding.

When he was a teenager, did I want to kill him? Yes,
But all parents feel that way.
Did he give me grey hair and challenge me daily?
Yes, of course he did.
Do I have any regrets on the matter?
No, of course I do not.

When I first held my daughter, in my arms, as she rested on
my chest,
Nothing can describe the feeling of overwhelming love
That I felt at that moment, and all the moments afterwards.
Watching her grow up and became a woman, is quite beautiful.

She was like sponge, absorbing all kinds of information
At record speed.
Her eyes sparkled when she would see something,
Curious as a girl could be.
She sang with such perfect pitch, danced when we danced,
Played and learned, and grew to be decent and outstanding.

When she was a teenager, did I want to kill her? Yes,
But all parents feel that way.
Did she give me grey hair and challenge me daily?
Yes, of course she did.
Do I have any regrets on the matter?
No, of course I do not.

Nothing can describe the overwhelming feelings of pride
that I have,
For both of my children are remarkable and
responsible people.
My son extended his family and married a remarkable
and beautiful,

Janean Phillips

Talented and courageous woman.
They travel, they have many friends, they work and they play.
I have no doubt that they will take care of each other.

No mother could be more proud.
No mother could have more joy.

My daughter extended her family and married a remarkable
and beautiful,
Talented and courageous man.
They have extended their family even farther,
Having perfect and wonderful,
Beautiful, funny and creative daughters.
My granddaughters.
They travel, they have many friends, they work and they play.
I have no doubt that they will take care of each other.

No mother could be more proud.
No mother could have more joy.

Nothing can describe the overwhelming feelings
Of love that I have for them.
Nothing can describe the overwhelming need for sleep.
Nothing can describe the overwhelming possibilities
Of the adventures to come,
As I travel, have many friends, work and play,

In this next chapter of mine.

I have lived a full life and
Nothing can describe my curiosity of what's next.

LAYMAN'S TERMS:
STREAM OF THOUGHT

Momma used to tell me, "Why go looking for trouble?"
Whenever I would go see my doctor.
She hadn't been to the doctor in years,
And for many, many years, she did live.

I would still visit my doctors, for various reasons,
And rush to call her for the newest
Comments, diagnoses and strange ten-dollar words
That the doctor would add to my chart.

Granuloma means skin, so why not just say Skin?
The Circle of Least Confusion is not just the world that I
live in...
But it is in reference to vision, where everything
Is equally in and out of focus.

Out of focus, indeed.

The Prognosticators should use Layman's terms, she
would cite.
But instead they want the common man
To just lay down their knowledge
And never question those who are in practice.

At Whitt's End

I have refused to lay down, in addition to being told to
Slow down as I have gotten older.

I've questioned many a doctor, and have fired just as many.
I was told by a friend, to never question those
Who have earned a degree and therefore, she assumed
Knew better than I.

I have a thickening of the heart. What does that mean?
So she tells me not to worry, until after I get older.
Of course my heart is thickening, as if to say: I am
Building up a wall, a fortress, so I cannot get hurt again.
How fitting.

IBS is what? Irritable Bowel Syndrome?
Something very common, for the common man,
And something we suffer from, due to stress.
You mean Irresponsible Bout With the Senseless.

Great! Stress is something that can kill me!
I was asked to find ways of eliminating stress,
So I figured the only way to do that, was to die.

Fat Necrosis, you say? Is that a good or a bad thing?
For weight loss is what I had experienced,
Much to my happiness.

But was told that I could stand to lose even a few more pounds.

Even at 114 pounds, how can he say that I was
considered Obese?
I have been fighting genetics all of my life.
And fighting idiot doctors, as well.

My flat feet have never stopped me from dancing.
My genetic pooch has never stopped me from dancing.
My curved lower Lumbar has never stopped me from dancing.
That curve has afforded me to be able to do all kinds
of acrobatics.
And even at fifty-one, I am still able to do cartwheels.

And Yes, I still do cartwheels.

The Center of Intellect, De Novo, Back of the Feet.
Of course!
So I changed my Diet, of Food and Knowledge,
And have learned what I can and cannot have,
What I can and cannot tolerate,
What I decide that I will understand and learn...

So Toxicity is what one needs of which to get rid,
Whether it be mineral, vegetable or animal.

AT WHITT'S END

I need not to be talked to, with such
Persnickety Jargon.
Just say what's on your mind,
And temporarily cure me from this disease called Death.

Will my certificate say, that I did nothing in this life,
But sit, get Arthritic, get Elderly and Drool?
No, it will not.

It will say, that I lived a great life, with
Vibrant Colors, a Grand Taste for Life and Satiation,
Excitable Curiosity, Adventure, Fantastic Artistry,
And Unconditional Love,
With Brilliant Creativity and Unending Kindness
And Patience.
And plenty of close friends, to back that up...

I will continue to live like the child from within.
Do not talk Down to me,
Just talk TO me.

So, Momma, why go looking for trouble?
I do not.
Sometimes, it comes looking for me.
And, I am always ready.

THE ART OF ANIMAL HUSBANDRY

My eyes and my thoughts are bombarded with
Images of beautiful women, of how to make up my face,
Fit bodies, large breasts, expensive colorful clothing,
Large hair, and fingernails that scream "I do not work for
a living."

And reminders that the clock is ticking.

What is all this imagery for?

It is geared toward the beautiful people,
To stay that way and catch a mate.
I have nothing to offer, and haven't learned to fish,
So why try?

This is the Art of Animal Husbandry,
Of which I have failed miserably.
I tried it once, at too young of an age,
And it did not take.

At too young of an age, it is NOT supposed to take,
For I have not yet earned all of my stripes.
But as I have aged,
It is most expected and I am doomed a failure,

If I do not get it right the second...or even, third...time.

Is this what life is supposed to be about?
I have added to the population!
I have earned my stretch marks!
I have earned my grey hair!
I have earned my wrinkles and cellulite!

THESE things SHOULD be considered beautiful,
In which they are very unique to me,
Unique to everyone, who has carried these
Battle scars!

Life is a battle, yes?

A fight to the end, a fight to the finish.
The one with all of the stripes wins!
So it would be more than nice,
To have a war-mate along the way.

And yet,

I have yet to find that comrade who is strong enough,
That barracks mate who is patient enough,
To continue on this battle until the end, with me.
So far, no one has been worthy in this

Elusive Animal Husbandry.

These animals are looking for the perfect colors
That I cannot provide.
These animals are seeking independently wealthy
Mates, when they themselves are poor of everything else.
They believe they are entitled to perfection,
When they are so far from perfect.

They, too, have been bombarded with this imagery,
So I find that I cannot blame them,
Nor can I find the time to fight them.
So, have I lost the battle?

No, not quite yet.

Patience is in the Art of Animal Husbandry.
Confidence is in the Art of Animal Husbandry.
Education, Knowledge, Curiosity...
Thirst, Adventure, Experience...
Are all the stripes that I have earned and will continue to earn,
As I continue to educate myself on the Art of
Animal Husbandry.

BRACE FOR IMPACT

The storm is not coming, it is already here.
I have fallen off of a cliff,
And there was no way to save myself.
Nowhere to hide.

I was not prepared, no time to think.
It came out of nowhere,
And hit my home like a ton of bricks.
I was pelted.

This tornado came in the form of a male,
Whereas I fell in the moment of an encounter
Of a perfect combination of humor, conversations,
Smile, availability and comfort.

I had built up an intentional wall,
Necessary from storms, wars and mistakes too harsh
to forgive.
And with one wave, one motion,
This tempest blew in from all directions and knocked me over.

I did not recognize it at first.
I was not sure of what was happening.
There was a strange throbbing that resonated

Throughout my body, swirling, fighting,
Then exited every inch.

I was frozen for a moment, as the cold took my breath away.
Then I began to get warmer, as I fought off this storm.
I did not want to fall, but I allowed myself to get caught.
Where is my wall, my fortress,
And where did my soldiers go hide?

I was unprepared for the severity of the storm.
I had fallen off of a cliff,
And there was no way to save myself from the impact.

HE SINGS AND DANCES

He has the face that only a mother could love,
But he sings like Johnny.
This is no matter to the women who fawn over him,
For such things are truly unimportant.

He has the body and height of a garden gnome,
But he dances like Adam and Trace.
This is his winning grace and hidden talent,
For such things help with getting by.

He has no hair, he has tons of hair,
He is tall, he is short,
He is wealthy, he is poor,
He is ugly, he is beautiful.
But he sings and dances like Toby,
Brad,
Kenny,
Dwight,
Josh and Keith.

His deep, passionate voice makes the hearts burst.
Even men are drawn to him, for he moves and sings
With soul, familiarity and compassion.
And the swooning begins.

His talent is God-given,
His love for music is innate.
He gave birth to his baby,
Raised it with love,
Nurtured it and gave it to the world.

He is unselfish, for he sings
And he dances, like Elvis.

CRYSTAL

You had rage against me, unprovoked, unwarranted
and unwelcome.
It is crystal clear, that you have no concern for me.

You took your frustrations of your life out on me,
And verbally bitch-slapped me.
It is crystal clear, that you do not care about me.

You were my friend once, we did everything together,
I reached out to you, you ignored me, you had excuses for me,
It is very crystal clear, that you no longer want me around.

On some days, I feel like I am expensive crystal glass,
That at any moment, if you drop me,
I will break.

On other days, I feel like I am expensive leather, with a
strong hide and spine,
And at all other moments, you beat me down,
Until you think I will become soft and pliable.

Mostly, I am somewhere in between.

You called me over, we talked,

And then you told me to Shut Up...
You called me over, we talked,
And then you insulted my very existence.
You called me over, you made love to me,
And then you never called again.

It is crystal clear, that you do not love me,
For if you loved me, you would recognize, appreciate, be strong,
And you would want to be in between
The crystal and the leather.

I am expensive crystal, and I will no longer break.
And that should be very crystal clear.

MASK

I have forgiven myself for all and any of the mistakes that I
have made.
Once forgiven, I was freed from the burdens that hold my
shoulders down.

Forgiving others is quite the other story.
And Forgiving others who intentional hurt you
Is a challenge of epic proportions.

Truly, you must admit, that once you let something go,
It does not stay gone forever.
But yet, it lingers in the compartments and tiny rooms
Of your fascinating brain.

A sight, a smell, a moment in time...
A location, a memory, a sound,
Are all it takes, for the floodgates to open.
It is quite difficult to remember the fun times,
If there were any.

Once someone has hurt you, you take all the time that
you need
To heal, to recover, to pick up the pieces of your scattered soul.
You are entitled to the amount of recovery that you

deem necessary.
Sometimes, when living in Ohio, a piece of your soul may
be found
In Colorado, in Tennessee, and/or in Europe.

I have been hurt, and I am sure, without a doubt, you have
been too...

I do not wear a mask, as much as I think you think I do.
However, once you had decided that it was about time for
you to
Remove yours, I discovered a hideous creature behind it.

You revealed yourself slowly, continuing to elude me with false
Kindnesses, false comments and phony compliments.
And now, I must say, "Boy, you were good!"
And in addition, I must say,
"I feel very sorry for you."
Man, Oh man, how your smile was deceiving...

Hug me? How dare you!
For just moments ago,
You stabbed me in the back, by lying to others about me.
High five? You must be kidding!
For moments ago,
You stole from me and tried to get me into trouble.

AT WHITT'S END

Smile at me?
Greet me?
Ask how I am doing?
Truly, it is more than small talk that you want.

You want another stab at me, don't you?

What are you expecting others to see, as you keep that
mask off?
Do you wear your mask at home, as you yell at your children,
And as you boss around your family?
Do you wear your mask at work, as you successfully lie about
everything?
Do you wear your mask while out and about, finding ways
to never reveal
The true You?

Your mask is moldy, rotting and ugly.
It is growing and growing and it may be too late
For you to be safe from it.
You are far from perfect and it is quite okay.

I must forgive that hideous creature behind that mask,
As well as staying far from it.
You are the devil, and I wonder if you know it.

The devil may wear designer labels,
But she also wears motorcycle clothing.
The devil may fool you into believing that she is a teacher
and she may
Sport a cute little hair style,
But she also wears it to hide those thorny horns.
The devil may be overweight,
But it is because of all the little children she has eaten.

It is I...who must forgive those devils and do my damnedest
to forget.
And yet, I can see, I can hear, but I can also forgive and heal.

MY MOTHER, MY FATHER, I THANK YOU

You have not only given me life,
You have given me the power
To use my creativity for the good.

Because of you, I am kind, I am giving,
I am patient and I am forgiving.
Forgiving of myself for my shortcomings,
Forgiving of others, who judge me too harshly,
For not getting to know the real me.

My parents were never up on a pedestal,
And never put me there either.

When I was younger, my mother would put me
On top of the dryer, lean down to meet my eyes
And talk with me, one on one, heart to heart.
She spent time with me, helping me with homework,
And nurse my wounded soul, when others were mean to me.

She taught me to cook, to clean, to organize and much more,
And to accept everyone, no matter what.

My parents were never up on a pedestal,
And never put any of us children there either.

When I was younger, my father would come home,
Dinner would be ready, with eleven souls around the table,
Food was consumed, jokes were told, then we would
Digest and focus, on the light of candles, meditating
To the sounds on the record player console.

He taught me to be patient, study, learn all that I could, and
much more,
And to accept everyone, no matter what.

Church was fun, I sang the loudest.
Church was too serious at times, for I had to make up sins
to confess.
School was interesting, with a variety of kids from
the neighborhood,
Walking past the Mercy Woods, telling tales of ghosts
and hippies.
School was fun, most of the teachers were kind and memorable,
I became resilient, especially having to walk one to two
miles each way,
Even in the harshest of climates.

Halloween was exciting, running from door to door, being safe
And having fun with the other kids, comparing costumes,
Organizing and counting candy.
I am surprised I didn't have more cavities.

Cortland apples and powdered donuts bring happy memories
to me,
Even to this day.

We survived the Blizzard of 1978, although we stayed home
From school for many days.
Against my mother's wishes,
We layered ourselves to play outside in the snow.
We survived the many storms that caused the
creek at the top of the street to overflow.

We played Hide-And-Seek block-wide, with what seemed like
Hundreds of kids running about,
As the parents sat on porches and helped with the perfect
hiding spot.
We survived flying down the snowy Suicide Hill,
On old rickety sleds and old, cracked plastic snow discs.

My parents were never up on a pedestal,
Nor were we children,
For if we had a pedestal, I am sure that it would have
been broken,
With all of the fighting and disagreements
That went on in our home.

Soccer and baseball, fun with park leaders, with

Hundreds of kids playing Duck, Duck, Goose,
And Boy Scouts, Girl Scouts and festivals at church and school,
Are all fond memories to me.

Many Christmases, that I now know they could not afford,
Never went by without a gift of some kind.
A tangerine and gum in our stockings,
Along with a bowlful of walnuts
And a bowlful of ribbon candy and chocolate.
All nine would wait at the top of the stairs,
Then barrel down to see what was under the tree.

I believe that one main goal of parenting
Is to make your child as independent of you as possible,
As well as, to educate, have fun, to make them safe
And have them be kind, informed,
And productive human beings.

If this is the truth, my mother and my father have done
Their job right, for the most part.

It is amazing to me, that with all of us in one household,
That our parents did not kill us and bury us in the backyard.
For that, I am forever grateful.
Thank You.

EXPRESSION / IMPRESSION

What is your form of expression,
To let everyone know that you are here,
That you are entitled to validation,
That you create, so in order to be seen?

Dance, to the sounds on the radio,
To the live bands, at dance clubs and
A variety of venues, showing the world
That you are here.

Sing along with the songs
In your car, at concerts, and at home,
Playing your favorite music,
Letting the world know
That you are here.

Paint on canvasses, plain 'ole pieces of paper,
Blocks of wood, or on metal or on walls,
Using dazzling colors, along with stripes,
Swirls, polka dots and zigzags,
Creating anything and everything
For the world to see
And enjoy
And ponder.

Get painted, with make-up, along with gloss
For your hair, your fingernails,
Wonderful hues of a variety of colors,
Of a variety of clothing,
To embellish and celebrate the real you.

Dress up in costumes galore,
Have fun at Oktoberfests, on Halloween,
At Renaissance fairs, festivals,
And at Girls Night Out, with hats and boas,
Drinking chocolate martinis and
Celebrate your life
And the lives of your family and friends.

Write, to your heart's content,
Tell the world what you want, think, feel, see and do.
Let the world know that you are here, with kind words,
Gentle words, words of persuasion,
Statements that make the masses think,
Statements that make one cry,
Because they can identify with it,
And harsh words, to get your point across.
Write what you know, share what you feel,
And express what you are missing.

Express yourself with your choice of tattoos galore,
Or just one,
Anywhere on your body, everywhere on your body,
To let the world know...or just one person know,
That you are creative, expressive,
Adventurous and soulful and leaving a lasting impression,
because
You are here.

EPIPHANIES FROM MANY TIFFANIES (1)
FROM BOSTON: DEAR BEAU, I FINALLY GET IT

Your honesty is appealing
The others were never upfront, honest or even caring.
You are toxic, poison to me.
Your alcohol and cigarette addictions
Are your weaknesses that you cannot seem to combat.

My addiction is you.

I am watching you kill yourself and I wish I knew why.
You hate yourself so much that you are willing to
sacrifice yourself
In front of your loved ones.
You come across confident
But you are compensating for fear.

Somehow, you know that I'd never let you down,
That I'd never cheat,
That I'd stand by you,
No matter what.

But since you've always known heartache,
Cheating and lying and mistrust,
You are comfortable with that in your life.

At Whitt's End

You will keep me at a distance on purpose
Because I represent hope,
Unending patience and understanding
And you believe that you don't deserve any of that.

You are basically non-judgmental.
You say what's on your mind,
Including that you love me,
That I'm beautiful and smart,
Funny and honest and that my honesty and confidence
Are what makes me so sexy and beautiful.

I am fixated on you because of that statement alone.

No man has ever been this honest, this direct,
Although I do not believe everything that you say.
You were physically not selfish in the beginning.
You introduced me to your friends, then took them away.

You shared stories with me that I can't be a part of
And that makes me sad,
Jealous, confused and disappointed.
You are very attractive to me and I've never had that.
The others were Trolls.

Janean Phillips

I wonder why you'd ever be
Remotely attracted to me.

Ultimately,
You cannot be trusted.

113

EPIPHANIES FROM MANY TIFFANIES (2)
FROM LAKE MARY: DEAR GUY, YOU FEAR ME

I know I'm cute, but not beautiful,
As I know you think you see beauty.
I am kind, giving, devoted
And dedicated and loyal,
And still, never enough for you.

You fear me, because I would never let you down.
You want to surround yourself with aesthetic beauty,
Never looking too deeply
Because you would find yourself there
Within those discovered deep recesses
Of selfishness and shallowness.

Of course I do not know the future, but I will outlive you
Because you will be cancer-ridden with toxins.
And when that happens, you will need someone
To warm your heart, hold your hand,
Reassure you...as you venture into the vast unknown.

I am that person, now.

I feel stuck on you because I sense that you love me.
Your beauty and knowing smile,

Janean Phillips

Humor and charm,
Devotion to your kids and friends,
And your animated story-telling,
Are all those things that make me feel
Warm, safe, comfortable, wanted,
Cherished, desired and yearned for...
In your company.

Why you won't share and extend that
Into the many aspects of your life,
Beyond our late rendezvous,
Is continuously upsetting and baffling.

As I told you, I have a self-diagnosed
"Disease" of tolerance and hope
And that is some of the reasons why
I can't let go.
I never let go of anyone.

That says to me that I don't care enough
About myself,
That you don't care about me,
That you never will,
And that my well-being is not important to you.

I feel that you do love me and you do fear me.

You are just lying to yourself.

EPIPHANIES FROM MANY TIFFANIES (3)
FROM MONROE: DEAR ROBERT, YOU STILL CAN DROWN IN THE SHALLOW END

You don't call to check on me.
Do you want to?
Do you wonder and worry about me,
Like I do you?

Jokingly, you say that you'd marry
A wealthy, terminally-ill, 95-year old woman,
Service her occasionally until she died,
Then live off of her money, for the rest of your life.
So wealth is really what you are after?
This makes you selfish and shallow.

If I was wealthy, or at least better off
Than I am today, or better off than I have been
All of my life, you would consider me an option?

This I now know.

Should I want to be with a man
Who thinks this way?
I have realized that I have never truly been
Deeply loved by any man.

I have discovered that I have
At least two flaws:
I never get mad
And I never hate.

I get upset, sad and disappointed,
But never mad or hate.
Perhaps I should tell myself to get
Mad at you and hate you.

Then perhaps I would heal faster
From this life-changing
Heartache and heartbreak.

What is it in me that senses out men like you
...and why do I feel that I have to save men
Like you?

Perhaps I somehow know
That these relationships are doomed to fail,
For my fear of something.
But what do I need to be afraid of?
Why do I need a family?

What did you fear?
What DO you fear if you allow me to get to know you

And your family and let me into more of your life?

What harm am I inflicting on myself
By having hope in a hopeless situation?

It seems that I am the one who is drowning
As long as I stay in the shallow end.

EPIPHANIES FROM MANY TIFFANIES (4)
FROM ST. XAVIER: DEAR JONAH, THIS IS WHO I AM

How can I have faith in myself,
When no one else does?
It is amazing to me how one person
With their unfounded, insensitive comment
(one glance, one summing up, one thought)
Can strike me down,
Verbally kick me,
Damage my spirit
And burst my bubble...

When this occurs, it prevents me
From functioning like a normal human being.
I have been wondering why I am like that...
Why am I so sensitive?

It is those things within me that make me
Who I am,
That some people can only take in small doses
And for that matter,
Not at all.

Even on most days, I cannot stand my own company.

Janean Phillips

I have been deeply betrayed, abandoned, by you,
And have never felt more alone, today,
Than any other day, in all of my 40 plus years.

I can't stop crying and punishing myself
With sappy American novels, foreign films
And French independent movies.
Trying to get a better understanding
Of myself, my place in this life,
And knowing my purpose, is most difficult,
Since I am unfocused.

So far, no breakthrough.

With all of these three wasted months
Since you gave up on me,
I am no closer to understanding me,
But have come closer to almost hating
All men, for all of their betrayals,
Their lying, their cheating, seducing,
And physical harm, that has been
Portrayed to me, in motion and in print,
Within the confines of my small space
That I currently dread and occupy.

At Whitt's End

My bed has become my tentative salvation,
As I curl up and try to read about the lives of others.
My couch has become my companion,
As I sit, lean and curl up, and as I try to stay awake
And watch the heartache that unfolds before me.

I am getting older by the minute,
And I still keep making the same mistakes.

But are they mistakes or just educational
Steps along the way?
Perhaps I am not to question the Why of me,
But to just recognize that this is THE me
That I supposed to come to love and enjoy.

This is just who I am...

EPIPHANIES FROM MANY TIFFANIES (5)
FROM DALLAS: DEAR CHRISTIAN, DID YOU GET A SPEEDING TICKET?

We made love and I cried again,
But you didn't seem to mind.
I can do that with you, be vulnerable,
Weak and embarrassed,
Excited...and it doesn't seem to bother you.

The others had NO room for that.
Why?

That's also the appeal.
What were you expecting to happen
After we've spent this much time together?
It was inevitable, for me, to fall.

How could you not feel the same,
As we shared so much, physically and emotionally?
We've seen each other cry...

Did your friends not like me?
Did they influence your decision,
Because you feel that we are not
In the same league?

AT WHITT'S END

I truly enjoyed them,
And I do miss them all.
Was it your mother who helped influence your leaving me?
I knew that she didn't like me, after she heard that I
had children.

Are One Night Stands, where I am headed,
In order to be touched?
How long can I go without being touched,
Until my heart builds a permanent wall
And my soul shuts down forever?

I have discovered that I am a Doormat,
A set of Stepping Stones,
A Bridge over a Gap,
A Teacher,
And a live Speed Bump.
Whereas, these men, like YOU,
That I have allowed into my life,
Step over me when they are done,
Step on me when they are done,
Learn from me, gain some sort of confidence
That they were lacking, and leave when they are done.

They drive over my body, heart, mind and soul,
And dash onto the next thing that appeals to them.

That indicates to me, without true reasoning,
That I am nothing more than garbage to them,
As they speed away onto bigger things.

Does that say more about me...
Or more about them?

I would have to say, with as much honesty as possible,
That that would be the choices of both parties involved.
I am no longer available to be driven over,
So you are done taking out the trash...

IRA'S APARTMENT

A phone call from a friend and I dashed over
To help clean up Ira's apartment,
For Ira was no longer there.
The beginning of some sadness for me.

Ira was elderly and perhaps a little jumpy.
Ira suffered a malady
And was never to return,
Although he voiced his wants.

As I cleaned and cleared,
Over several weeks and weeks,
I came to know Ira, from multiple
Correspondences that he saved for years.

He was kind, giving,
Sometimes confused,
But very clear and precise
In his requests for justice,
And in his compliments and generosity.

He requested to return to active duty,
He requested better-timed traffic lights,
He requested letter-writing dialogue,

Which made me all the more sad,
Wondering if he was just quite lonely.

I cleared out his vast collections of
Radios, electronics, flashlights,
Cameras, batteries, antiques, etc.
It was the etcetera which seemed quite endless.

A collection that I supposed began in his
Youth, some seventy years prior.
A collection of Ira's life...

While cleaning out his kitchen,
I truly broke into tears
When faced with bloated cans of soup
And stale boxes of food,
Dating back to 1985...

Mostly being quite selfless, my thoughts
Went to my future and my need for contact,
So I could envision a life without human touch.
Ira did not have a wife or children.
He kept everything, so what was he missing?

I threw away things, I boxed things
And when I found photos and letters to

And from England, and papers I deemed
Of most importance, I saved those things
To give to his only living two relatives,
Living in far away Oregon.

My friend helped out and spoke of Ira
With such kindness and compassion.
I shared with her my findings and
She shared stories of Ira,
Which made me feel that I got to know him.

The apartment was finally cleared and cleaned.
With new carpet, new air and heat,
Fresh paint and a new kitchen floor,
New bathroom and a new resident.

Nightly, as I sat in my new home,
Thankful and grateful for my new surroundings,
I prayed for the soul of Ira.
I never got to meet him
And became additionally sad
When I heard of his passing.

Am I doomed to the same fate?
I asked myself, as my head hit my pillow each night.
Somehow, I already knew that answer.

Janean Phillips

Perhaps Ira was whispering to me
To continue to live my life as I was already
And to continue to reach out to others
As I do daily...

Despite being gone from this Earth,
Ira is in the energy of this apartment.
He lived here for many years
And he will continue to live within
The hearts and memories
Of those who truly knew him.

129

CHRISTINA'S GRANDFATHER

My Grandfather was a great man.
Everyone who knew him,
Knew that he would give you
The shirt off of his back,
And also would never make you feel bad
For that generous and unselfish act.

Thinking about my many wonderful childhood
Memories with him,
My Grandfather was always on the floor
Letting us ride his back like a horse.

He had a great sense of humor
And was a gentle soul.
When I would go visit my Grandparents,
My Grandfather would sneak away to a
Fast-food place close by and get me a meal,
Because I didn't want whatever Grandmother
Had cooked that day.

I have fond memories of going to the race track with him,
Where he would let me bet on the horses,
Based on the horse's names.
When he would buy lottery tickets,

Janean Phillips

He told me that our tickets could not touch
Because the luck would run off of them.

During many summers, I would go fishing with him.
He would bring extra worms, because he knew
That I was going to get upset and set some of the worms free,
So they could find their families.

He taught me how to ride a bike.
He taught me how to drive.
He let me take puffs off of his cigar.

Then in September, he was diagnosed with Pancreatic cancer,
Giving him a Death sentence of less than nine months.
However, we had less time together than we had hoped.

My young son and I were at the hospital,
Then at a rehab nursing home,
Every day
To see him, spend time with him and talk.

Even with as much pain that he was in,
He let me know that I had brought him much joy into his life.
As I walked over to his bed and as he stroked my hair,
He told me that he was proud of me.

AT WHITT'S END

Having that last moment with him
And with how bad as it was,
He spoke of being ready to be
With Grandma.
He said to me, "I had a very good day with you."

My Grandfather died on 10/10/14.
My Grandmother had died on 4/10/10.
I took comfort in knowing that they were now together.

As I was going through mementos at his home,
I found my Grandmother's journal.
She said that she knew that they were going to last,
That they just had to get past a year of arguing.
She knew that they would be soul mates forever.
She knew that their marriage would work, no matter what.
They were best friends and she knew that when she died,
Their love would never die.

I knew that my Grandparents loved to travel.
Their last trip together was at Yellowstone National Park.
They got lost while in the park and relied on
Grandmother to get them out.
She had read the map wrong and Grandfather
Had driven into a lake.

Nearer to his death, when he was at his own home,
And in and out of a coma,
Grandfather talked about a map,
Pleading with Grandma to "read the map right this time."
I now know that he had only two options
To meet up with her, and relied on her
For the right directions.

Somehow I knew that Grandmother was there
With us, all along.

As I continued to go through his things,
I found lots of maps and plenty of photos
Of their travels together.
Again, I take comfort in knowing that they
Will be together and travel whenever
And wherever they want.

I am glad that things had happened this way.
I believe that my Grandfather knew that
Waiting nine months to pass away
Would have been horrible for me to witness.

At his military funeral, it was so quiet
That you could hear a pin drop.
I remember the crisp, snap sounds of the folding of the flag,

AT WHITT'S END

The salutes from everyone in dress uniform
And the disciplined composure of the soldier who
Handed me the flag, even though I was bawling.

I will continue to have wonderful memories of him,
Even while he was being taken care of with Hospice at home,
As the military personnel had come into his living room,
Pinned him,
Saluted him,
And thanked him for his service.

My Grandfather was a great man.

MY HAIR SMELLS LIKE BACON

At the age of fifty, I never thought
That I would be asking,
"Would you like fries with that?"
I am a short-order grandmother
Who was a short-order cook.

I have been a gypsy all of my life.
I cannot sit still, I cannot stay
In the same place all the time,
I love to move around,
Dance and talk,
Learn, see, and do...

Needing a change and needing a chance,
I applied for a job at a local motorcycle tavern,
To be the lunchtime cook and to run the kitchen.
I wasn't sure why I was hired, except that perhaps
They were desperate and so was I...
Plus I was wearing a fantastic pushup bra!

As I made the kitchen my own,
I organized and labeled the wares, canned goods,
And everything else.
I could barely reach the microwave and they

Had to lower the speed rail by three inches,
To accommodate my five foot frame.
That kitchen was definitely in need of a woman's
Touch...and was most definitely run by a man.
Poorly...

I was on time, but almost daily
The owner was always late.
This set me back by anywhere
From 20 to 30 minutes.
But I had to bust my ass in the kitchen
While he sat his down at the bar
For a morning beer.

I kept saying to myself that this lifestyle
Is so foreign to me, but I needed the work.
As usual, I gave it my all
And I became friends with the cute
Bartenders and wait staff.

I was civil to the barflies and tavern trolls,
Because I had to be.
Some of them were funny and great
Story tellers, but also some of them
Gave me the creeps.

Janean Phillips

Every damn day I had to cook bacon,
Along with preparing the daily specials.
Being the nurturing type, one day
I suggested chicken salad and
A fruit plate, expecting horrible comments.

I was surprised that that daily special
Took off...and it somehow became a hit
Amongst the patrons, even just for the day.
Now bear in mind, that I truly cannot cook,
But I wanted to try something new and healthy.
After that day was over, it was back
To cooking bacon again...

After work each day, I would run errands.
I ran to the grocery store, the hardware store,
The post office, the bank, etc.
Each time, I was approached by various men.
They would ask my name, sometimes for my
Phone number, but mostly we would just talk
About a variety of things, giving me the false
Impression that they were interested in just
Little old me...

One day, as I was just coming home, my neighbor
Stopped me to have small talk about the weather.

At Whitt's End

He was a slight, harmless, little old man, as white
As the snow, with a funny gait and slumped shoulders.

Unfortunately, we had to get real close,
In order for him to hear me, or so it seemed.
As he got closer, he actually sniffed my hair.
I was taken aback and looked at him funny
Enough for him to respond.

He told me that I smelled fantastic, and plus he wanted
To know what the scent was, that was wafting
Around my crown...
I told him that I wasn't wearing any perfume,
So I grabbed a chunk of my auburn hair
And proceeded to take a sniff.

An epiphany and an "Oh my god!" later,
I realized that it was the bacon.
My hair smelled like bacon, so that is why
I was being pursued, so to speak, by various men,
At various venues, for various things that they wanted,
I was sure...

Now, I had two choices: To get mad or get creative.
So I chose the latter.
I sat in my sparse, lonely apartment thinking of ways

That this situation could benefit everyone.
Was I upset that my charm and wit,
Cute, youthful looks and dazzling smile,
Were not the reasons why I was approached
By ugly and hot guys alike?
Only for a minute.
Chemistry is an interesting creature.

As I continued to work and cook bacon daily,
I continued to attract men at every place that I went after work.
While doing so, I invited them to partake in
The fantastic food at the tavern and for them
To come and enjoy the festivities and music.

More and more new patrons frequented the tavern.
More and more, the menu expanded, the word got out,
More local bands wanted to play there,
And as the place expanded, so did the owner's wallet.

Little did the owner know that I was pumping
The Scent of Bacon into the air system,
And little did the wait staff and bartenders know
That I was spraying Scent of Bacon onto their hair.

Everyone was happy with the success of the tavern.
Everyone was happy to be there, listen to great music,

At Whitt's End

And to eat unhealthy and healthy foods.

When my gypsy spirit became restless again,
I knew my job was done and I moved on...
I worked at an art studio, an Irish Pub, a playhouse,
A motorcycle shop, a concert venue,
And the list goes on and on...
My hair no longer smells like bacon,
So perhaps it was my dazzling smile, after all.

COMPOUND FRACTURES (ANOTHER, NOT-SO-SHORT, NARRATIVE)

The sun was shining, not a cloud nearby,
Her windows were down and the top was off,
As Maggie drove down one road after another,
On her much needed vacation.

With the map on the passenger seat and with
The radio blasting, her hair was whipping in the wind.
A snack in her lap, munching away the day, she felt
Adventurous, courageous and whimsical.

She hadn't had a vacation in years.
She had just decided ONE day earlier to get out her map,
Spread it out on her living room floor and
Blindly picked a spot to vacate her life.

With one hand over her eyes and one hand
Twirling in the air, she place one finger down
And Voila! A mysterious place somewhere in
The middle of the great USA.

Maggie was very excited for she had
Never been in the middle before.
She had hurriedly packed a bag of clothes and

At Whitt's End

A bag of snacks, straightened up her apartment,
And did her damnedest to sleep before her adventure.

As she jetted down the road, an announcement
Got her attention, so she turned up the radio.
"Women are being kidnapped, left and right," it said,
In the area in which Maggie realized that she was driving.

Being a bit of the cautious type, she worried for a minute,
But then sloughed it off, feeling that she was in no danger.
She spied a general store alongside the road,
So she pulled over for refreshments and a potty break.

As she entered the antiquated store, the sound of the
Door clacking against the frame, and the sound of her
Shoes on the hardwood floor, brought fond memories
To her, as she reflected on long ago times with her grandparents.

She found a small basket and walked around, grabbing more
Snacks to munch on and she helped herself to a pop in
The small fridge by the front windows.
She tilted her head a bit, when she realized that it was
too quiet.

She approached the counter in the back
And was ready to tap the bell,

Whereas it seemed like out of nowhere
Appeared the elderly, disheveled clerk.

She said Hello to him and all he did was nod.
The hair on the back of her neck began to raise.
His eyes got bigger as he indicated with a tilt of his head,
"Run for the door"..."Run for your life."

Maggie hesitated for a moment, but did just that.
She dropped her things and ran, and within seconds
Someone was on her heels. Then darkness.
She knew that she had been grabbed by a male
And that he had placed a sack over her head.

She was thrown facedown into a van, her head still covered.
The man straddled her back and tied her hands.
With the van door still open, she could hear the clerk on
the porch.
He yelled, "Leave her alone." At that moment, Maggie heard
Many more male voices, with one saying, "Mind your own
business, old man."

Maggie listened intently. She heard muffled conversations,
Some laughter, some anger... When another male approached
The van, she deemed that he was the one in charge.
She felt as if she knew, that he was the one most to fear.

She realized that she could see a little through the holes in
the sack.
She could see at least seven men, all in camouflage, with lots
of guns.
Some were short, some were tall, some were bald and some
had tons of hair.
The one that she concluded was their leader, came back
over to the van.
She heard him state, 'The one who catches her, keeps her."
Maggie realized that she was now their prey, their target.

He gave directions to the other men and they complied.
They got into additional vehicles, then the van door closed.
The driver took off...and at that moment, Maggie felt
That her life could possibly end quite soon...

She had two options: Cry and Die, or Fight and Kill.
She chose the latter of the two...
She told herself that she would fight to the death,
And take out as many of those bastards as possible.
All she needed was a quick moment of freedom.

Maggie concentrated, as the van sped up one road and
down another.
They took many lefts and rights,
So much so, that she could not keep up.

She heard dull chatter on two-way radios.
The two men in the car remained eerily quiet, until the driver spoke.
He asked Maggie if she needed any water.

The other man voiced, "You have got to be kidding," continuing with
A reminder to him that she was their hostage, a possible mate,
And asked with a stern voice, "Why in the hell would you ask what she wanted?"
A slight argument ensued, as the driver tried to get his point across
That Maggie was also a human being.

The passenger smacked the driver on the back of the head, told him
To Shut Up and Drive, and that was what he did.
If given a chance, Maggie was going to try to target the driver for help,
She just didn't know how she was going to do anything at all.

Once at their destination and all of the vehicles stopped,
The van door flew open, Maggie was dragged out and thrown to the ground.
She heard their leader tell everyone to get ready...
The hood came off of Maggie's head. All of the vehicle's

headlights were on,
Bright against the darkness of the surrounding forest.

Maggie stood up, hesitant and a bit dreadful.
The leader came up to her, practically nose to nose,
Paused, then whispered, "Run."
He was slightly taken aback, when Maggie smirked. Then
he smirked.
Then Maggie turned on her heels and ran...
She had no idea where she was going, but she felt that at
any moment
She was going to be shot in the back.

She ran well, despite not seeing very well in the dark.
Her many years of jogging, kick-boxing, aerobics and yoga,
served her well.
She was a woman of many talents, creativity and she was a
woman to fear.
Maggie wanted to live and she was going to kill to do so...

Along the uneven terrain, she ran up a hill, being smacked
in the face
By low-lying branches. She felt as if her heart was going to
burst out
Of her chest, but she continued on, hoping to find a place to
hide, a place

Of respite, so she could strike one of them down with a large rock to the head.

Moments later, she found just a spot, behind a grove of trees, in and
Around a set of boulders. She put her shirt to her mouth to muffle her gasps.
In the background, she heard the men yelling and running, wondering where
She had gone. She could see the waves of flashlights, striped between trees.
She held her breath for a moment, so she could hear better.

She found a rock, held it firmly in her hand, and once one man got closer,
She nearly jumped on his back and slammed the rock at the base of his skull.
He went down as silently as she had been quick.
One down, she said to herself, not knowing just how many more there would be.

She ducked down and remained quiet, as more and more men got closer.
She ran as fast as she could, dodging the branches lit by the moonlight.
The stings on her face were intense, but she forged on...

She crested a hill and soon one man was on her heels.
She continued to run, feeling sure-footed, but he gained
on her,
Then tackled her to the ground.

She struggled, but he was able to force her onto her back.
He covered her mouth, put his mouth to her ear and told her
to trust him.
He whispered to her that he was undercover FBI and pleaded
with her
To go along with what was about to ensue.

She shook her head in agreement, and in doing so, he lifted
her to her feet,
Shot one bullet into the air, and yelled, "I've got her!"
All the men came running forth, whooping and hollering for
his success.
The men approached, smacking him on the back and shoulders,
And as he talked, basically puffing out his chest in
hunter-fashion,
She realized that he was the driver of the van.

The leader approached, placed a hand on his
shoulder, congratulated
Him and told him to do with Maggie what he deemed natural.
She was now his "captive," and was instructed to "take her"

that night.

Maggie got a bit sick to her stomach, thinking it was the trail mix and

Incessant running that effected her, not the foul
verbal comments

Coming out of the mouth of that damned, ignorant,
bully-of-a-leader.

Despite trying to control her physical reaction, she bent forward and puked,

Much to the amusement of the group of testosterone-driven trolls.

Maggie got angry, but controlled it, for she was going to go forth with her plan,

Come "hell or high-water" as her mother would say...

Grabbing her by the arm, her captor lead her back down the hill and

To a vehicle, where the other men were waiting.

Her captor put her in the passenger seat of his vehicle and sternly

Told her not to move. She complied.

He got into the driver's seat and away they went, caravanning to somewhere,

In the darkness, with headlights off.

Maggie kept her composure.

She asked, "How in the hell are you FBI?"
He questioned himself as to why he was even trusting her
not to tell,
But began to tell her that he had infiltrated this radical
group approximately
Six months earlier. He had lost contact with another agent
and was not
Sure how he was going to get out of this situation, nor how
it was all
Supposed to come to an end.

He told her that these horrible men have been
kidnapping vacationing
Women, holding them against their will, doing awful things
to them,
Making them tend the fields and cook, etc., in order for
them to continue
With their twisted beliefs and their agenda against
the Government.

Maggie listened intently, felt concern for him and eventually
asked him
About his agenda. "What are your plans for saving these
other women
And for stopping these men?" she asked. He told her that
he wasn't

Sure of what to do and how to do it, but with her help,
perhaps they could
Find the means to escape and get outside help. He told her
that she seemed
Like a fighter and that would benefit them in the long run...
Maggie reluctantly agreed, wondering about the real truth.

He looked at her fixedly and told her his name was Matthew.
She told him her name and they quickly smiled at each other.
Matthew asked her if she was ready for what was about
to happen,
And Maggie nodded...

When they got to the Compound, she had no idea of the
Scope of the situation. Once inside, she was overwhelmed
by the size of the
Borders of the her new, albeit temporary, prison. There
were men on every post, Men with guns at every exit and
entrance and rooftop. There was large field of Crops to her
left, rudimentary buildings scattered about, an unpaved
drive Throughout the compound and one main building
centered in the court.

As they got out of the vehicle, Matthew man-handled her on
purpose, to show off
His new prize. The other men exited their vehicles and

congratulated him again.

Their leader came up to him, nodded and then the men dispersed to different

Destinations. Matthew lead Maggie to his quarters, with his hand lightly gripping

Her arm. She finally believed the scope of the danger that he had portrayed to Her...and quickly prayed for reprieve...

As they entered the front door, she heard the distinct sounds of

Domestic violence... Men slapping women, women crying... women Screaming... And no one seemed to be bothered by it, except for the two of Them. She could feel his temperature rise as she stood next to him.

Once inside, he whispered to her that he did not believe that his place was Bugged or had any cameras, however, he wanted to reassure her that he meant Her no physical or mental harm. They sat on the edge of his bed, as he told her About joining the military and then the FBI...stating that he and another soldier Was chosen by their superiors to go undercover, learn all they could about this Group and within exactly four months to the day, the FBI was going to storm the Compound.

He continued on about losing contact with his partner while they were on another Twisted mission of grabbing more women. He did not know if he was alive or
Dead, but was told by the leader that his partner had decided to quit the group And left... All along the leader had stated that anyone could leave any time they Wanted, but most of the men behaved as if they sickly enjoyed their roles...

She listened and nodded, not knowing how to respond. Matthew gave her a
Look of concern, not knowing even if she could be trusted. He went into the Kitchenette, found a small snack and water and handed it to Maggie.
He told her that they would need to keep up the charade for a bit, as they
Secretly got the word out to the other women about their potential uprising
And escape. He firmly stated that several people will be killed, possibly
Including themselves. Maggie asked about children...and luckily there
Were none...

Matthew stated that if there were any listening devices in his home, they will
Be killed in their sleep that very night. He reassured her that

if anyone comes
Barreling inside his quarters at any time...he would do his damnedest to
Protect her...adding...that at that point she was on her own. He also stated
That for some reason, he knew that she could take care of herself.

"It is just way past time," he said, "for this crap to end."
Maggie held her snack in her lap, then finally had faith that it was not poisoned.
She ate heartily.
There was a knock on the door. She put the snack down, laid back on the bed,
Matthew winked at her and then opened the door. Her belongings had been
Placed on the threshold, obviously riffled through. Matthew grabbed them up And placed them on the floor by the door.

Maggie went over to her things, gathered some clothes, purposefully walked
Into the bathroom, closed the door and proceeded to take a shower.
Matthew had smirk on his face, indicating that he was impressed with her
Confidence and demeanor. He knew that she was the ally

that he had been

Hoping for... He knew that she was the one to help him save the others.

As Maggie quickly took her shower, she knew that she had to get

Her thoughts together, check out the Compound at daylight if possible, and

Find the Fractures in the perimeter of the Compound where she could escape.

It was quite possible that Matthew was delusional, she told herself, but somehow She knew better. She also knew that killing the leader was at the top of her

New agenda.

Maggie felt that she was possibly being videotaped in the shower, and also

Didn't seem to care. She was fit, strong, confident in her self-defense and

Fighting abilities, but she also knew that if she was attacked by more than

Five men at a time, she may not have a chance at living. Maggie was an

Ace Archer, had a Black Belt and also had handled guns before. She was

Positive that she could not afford to be too arrogant either.

Matthew seemed trustworthy, she told herself.

Maggie was done, got dressed and when she got out of
the bathroom,
Matthew was on the floor, with a pillow and blanket by the
front door.
He told her to take the bed, she complied, and as she laid
there, Matthew
Asked her where she was from and where she was going,
when they
Grabbed her. She asked, "Does it matter?" He told her that
it did not...
He told her to try to sleep well. As she drifted off for a bit,
she was
Making plans for the next day.

As Matthew arose, the sunlight was just barely coming into
the front window.
When he got up, he was surprised that Maggie was not in
the bed. He rushed
From room to room, then out the front door to find her. She
was sittng on the
Front stoop, with coffee in hand. To him, she looked
refreshed. He was
Taken aback that she was able to move around him without
making a sound.

She handed him her cup, stood up and told him that she wanted to know the
Layout of the Compound, wanted to know who could be trusted, how many people were there...and wanted to know where the guns were stored. He gave Her a puzzled look, whereas, as if to ask, "Who put you in charge?"

He smiled at her and told her everything that she wanted to know.

He drank the coffee, put the mug on the stoop, lightly grabbed her arm and took
Her to the fields. Maggie counted over twenty women, raking, picking
And gathering. He told her that this is where she needed to be each morning,
Then after that was done, the women gathered in the mess hall and cooked
For the men. Maggie dreaded this heathen mindset, but complied.
Quickly she noticed that the women did not talk to each other, so it was going
Be a challenge to gather information, as she gathered the food.

One of the women came over to her, handed her a basket and indicated what

Produce for her to pick. She did just that and moments later, a horn sounded.

Robotically and tragically, the women stopped what they were doing and like Zombies, they finished gathering and walked towards the mess hall.

"Holy shit!" Maggie said to herself...and followed the women.

Hurriedly, they went inside and began to prepare breakfast. Each of them

Had a specific duty, so Maggie felt like she was in the way. She was given

A tray of silverware, as the woman pointed to the tables. Maggie set the tables,

And watched as the women cooked, boiled, fried and sautéed everything.

Some of the women constantly cleaned, did dishes, chopped and stored

Items for the next meal and so on... Maggie observed, and was sick to Stomach, knowing that each of these women had been kidnapped, raped, Beaten and brain-washed into submission. Her task was more clear.

"These men must die," she murmured to herself. "They all must die"...

Over the next four days, the routine stayed the same. She was able to

Get some of the women to talk to her, as they ate their meals, after the men. They were rightfully cowardly, and whispered to her about where they were from, Where they were going, who they knew was worrying about them and how much They needed to get out of there. Maggie could see something in their eyes,
Collectively, beyond sorrow and pain. Their spirits were damaged, but not
Beyond repair. They were fighters like her...and she finally realized who
She could trust, which ones were the strongest...and which ones had
Possibly faced this kind of terror and abuse before.

She was confident in choosing just two women, confiding in them, and
Shared her findings with Matthew. Each day, after the mess hall was cleaned, The chores were done, and the daily exercises of combat training that they all Received, was over, Maggie was concerned that her plan would be thwarted.
She had to stick with her escape deadline, which she chose for two days
From then...and she had to believe that her plan would be carried out.

She knew that each night, they were forced to do things with their captors, they

Were being broken down every day...but she reminded them to hold onto the

Faith that they would return to their loved ones. But mostly, she told them to

Have confidence in knowing that they will be free, as they get justification in

Killing these heinous men. That seemed to be the clincher in her speech.

She gave the women and Matthew instructions, on a time and a place, of

Grabbing the guns, killing some of the men at various posts, grabbing a vehicle And driving through the front gates...to freedom. Matthew was impressed with

Her plan, but he, too, was worried that when the two women shared their plan

With some of their subordinates, they would be weak or traitors, out of fear.

Each night, as Maggie and Matthew had their pillow talk, they went over the

Plan, knowing that they could die. They had to believe that it would work

Or they would be enslaved forever. Escape was their only

hope. Matthew

Had to kill at least seven men, in a matter of minutes, to secure the vehicle

That would ultimately lead them to freedom, while Maggie had to kill just as Many to get to the gun shack. The two women and Maggie had been sneaking Some weapons to their quarters, after exercises, in order to use them on the Day of their escape.

During this entire time, Matthew had been having daily meetings with the

Leader and some of the other men, making plans for another kidnapping

Burst. Matthew shared with Maggie that plan. Since it was scheduled in

Just two days, that was the day that Maggie chose her plan to come to

Fruition. She was going to mend that Compound Fracture, in any and

All manner...that was humanly possible...

The next day went without a hitch, whereas the damn routine had stayed the Same. The escapees were keeping their ears to the ground, trusting that no one Would be a snitch and none of the enemy would be the wiser. The fields were Tended to, the chores were done, the men were fed,

the women were compliant,
The weather was a balmy ninety-two degrees... The plan
would go forth,
"Come hell or high-water," and Maggie and Matthew
were ready.

Just at dawn, when the dew was still fresh on the ground
and the sun was
Beginning to peak at the horizon, each of the two women...
and each of their Cohorts and comrades, attacked and killed,
and sliced and diced, strangled
And fatally maimed, their captors. It was quick, it was silent,
is was horrible
And it was necessary. As each of the women were done, they
exited their
Quarters, covered in battle blood and proud of what was
about to take place.

It was time... Maggie and Matthew arose, ready as ever,
weaponry in hand.
They wished each other luck, Matthew kissed Maggie on the
forehead and
Thanked her for helping him. He took a deep breath, ran out
the front door
And began shooting all of the men on the rooftops, all of the
men at posts,

And of course, they returned fired. Matthew's skills outmatched the dying men.

Maggie ran out of her quarters, going the opposite direction as Matthew.

She sprayed bullets into every man who was in her way. She ducked behind Barrels, vehicles, having only the sight of the gun shed as her main goal. Nothing was going to stop her from getting there. Nothing.

The silence of the morning quickly became loud chaos, as the unsuspecting

Men shouted orders to the others, to kill Matthew and Maggie upon sight.

There were explosions of gunfire in all directions, explosions of vehicles from

All over the Compound.

Men were being hit left and right. Maggie had no idea if Matthew or any of the

Women had survived and made it to safety. Maggie finally made it to the gun

Shed, reloaded her gun and grabbed more weaponry. Upon exiting the shed,

She came face to face with the leader. A one-to-one battle ensued. The leader

Was physically strong and was able to temporarily stun

Maggie with a punch to
The face... But she was quick and much smarter, skilled in
hand-to-hand Combat and was able to take everything that
he dished out.

Punches, falls, cuts and bruises... More punches, slams to
the side of the Building, choking, tripping... Then finally, as
Maggie and the leader were
Entangled, she was able to incapacitate the leader with one
stab to the liver.
She held him, nose-to-nose, as the look of surprise overcame
his face. She
Held him tightly, felt his body go limp, lowered him to the
ground, watched his
Eyes close and watched as he took his last breath.

No words were spoken. Maggie ran from the area to find
Matthew and the
Women at the east end of the Compound. She ducked behind
trees, dodged
More bullets, then spied Matthew near the entrance, which
was still heavily
Guarded. Matthew shot at more men, saw Maggie, jumped
into a vehicle and
Drove toward her. Maggie jumped inside. Matthew told her
that most of the

Women had made near the front, but ran back to some of the buildings for cover.

As they drove toward the front gates, Maggie stood in the vehicle's passenger

Doorway, held tightly to the frame and shot many men on the posts.

She quickly maneuvered herself into the passenger seat, as Matthew crashed

Through the front gates, at full speed. The metal twisted and flew in several

Directions, making a hideously deafening sound. Matthew drove like a bat out

Of hell...as both of them held their breath. As they continued to drive a fair

Distance to safety, they saw smoke billowing ahead of them, realizing that there

Were many vehicles barreling toward them. "What the hell?" Matthew

Exclaimed. "What the hell is that?"

Matthew slammed on the brakes, turned the car sideways and squinted against The sunlight to see what was coming at them. Maggie leaned forward to get a

Better look... It was the National Guard and the FBI, coming toward them in

Multiple assault vehicles. A helicopter flew overhead. Maggie
and Matthew
Quickly looked at each other, exited the vehicle and ran
towards their
Rescuers. Matthew saw his Commanding Officer get out of
the lead vehicle.

All of the lead vehicles came to a stop, but many more rushed
around them,
Kicking up dust, as they continued down the road to the
Compound.
Matthew rushed up to his CO and apologized for being out
of breath.
He had a puzzled look on his face, as he began to speak, but
his CO cut him off.
The other agents gathered around the two escapees, as the
CO shook Matthew's hand, then looked at Maggie.
The CO thanked Maggie for her help, as Maggie turned
to Matthew.
Matthew looked quite a bit more puzzled.
She looked at him and said, "I am FBI."
Matthew's jaw dropped.

She told him that she knew who he was on the day they met.
She had studied His file, learned of the kidnappings and had
been offered the chance to get word To him that the FBI was

storming the Compound. She had been sent into the County, where most of the women had been kidnapped and posed as a Vacationer, in order to get kidnapped herself.

Matthew was speechless.

As the dust settled around them, she continued with her story. She told him

That she decided not to tell him who she was and not to tell him of the

Pending rescue date, since it was the same date planned for the next

Kidnapping. She read his face, as she apologized to him for the secrecy.

He looked a little upset, but relieved as well.

Behind them, they heard a bit more gunfire, then silence. They turned and was

Relieved to see most of the women running toward them, alongside the other

Agents. Maggie ran toward them, hugging them collectively and one by one.

The agents ushered them into the waiting vehicles.

The two women, who helped with the escape, walked up to Maggie

And thanked her. The two women hugged

Each other, then walked arm-in-arm toward the safety of
a vehicle.

As the drama seemed to settle, Maggie turned toward her
CO, shook his hand, thanked him sarcastically for being on
time, then turned

To Matthew, who still had a puzzled look on his face. He
looked at his CO and

Asked, "My partner?" The CO shook his head and stated that
he was not sure

What happened to him, but feared that he was dead.
Matthew seemed to

Feel that as well. He turned toward Maggie and offered
his hand.

She put her hand in his, feeling his strength and seeing that
her hand was

So tiny compared to his. "You are an amazing woman,
Maggie," he said to

Her. He smiled and thanked her for her service and her help.
He had a serious look on his face, then asked her, "So, where
are you going

On your next vacation?"

She smiled and said, "Let's get out a map and see."

THE END

SPACE COWGIRL
BY JOHN PHILLIPS

Shauna has a secret
Close to her heart.
Fixed in the stars
Never to part.

Better than money
Greater than gold
The power of magic
Found in her soul.

No...not a man,
But a beast so great.
A sacred stallion
And the hour is late.

With bridle and mane
chute and swagger
She renders a call
And always he answers.

Biting her lip
She raises a hip
And smooth like silk

AT WHITT'S END

She slips...into the saddle.

With a nudge and a click
Away they will clip
Like the sail of a ship
Away she will slip...
On the back of her Cleveland Bay.

Hands on mane
She quickens the pace
And leads him to a shadowy place
Where salty sweat
Turns sugary sweet
When yesterday's sorrows
Melt in her sleep.

Under a moon and a blanket of stars
She's off to Venus, Jupiter and Mars.
Freedom's found flying through space
Exhilaration reigns...windswept face.

Where will they go?
No one will know
For Shauna has a secret
Close in her heart
And close does she keep it always.

DIVA MANTIA
BY JOHN PHILLIPS

Her gypsy spirit rises up
In a Caribbean seasick twist
The Diva Mantia saunters forth
As silky black magical mist.

Champagne glass
A touch of ice
Chopsticks in her hair
Smiling her swampy smirk
In the salty stardust air.

All hands run silent
Under the Kraken's stormy rage
But this daring daughter of Poseidon
Has foisted her cabin's cage.

She'll take your pain for pleasure
This martini mango flirt
Sporting a dangle bangle
In a silver miniskirt.

She nails the aquatic "bend and snap"
Upon this floating discotheque

At Whitt's End

Breaking hearts and dashing hopes
The teeth of the Hydra upon her neck.

Melon butt
Lemon breast
A tongue of tangerine
A mermaid's song
Yet a work of wraith
Oh! A sailor's aching dream.

Mariners, sailors and soldiers
All you men of courage be warned
This island gypsy with pirate's fire
Was the only soul
To weather out the storm.

COWBOY'S PLIGHT
BY JOHN PHILLIPS

On a Sonoran night
Under a windswept moon
When the Organ Pipe
Plays her solemn tune

O'er starlight
It's fight or flight
A cowboy's plight
An Arizonan nocturnal high noon

At campfire's coffee
A strong cigarette
When that spiny column
Casts a dark silhouette

His creeping hand
Forms a hangman's fist
Seizes your throat
Tightens his grip

Like the Reaper's cloak
Is this silent specter
So much so, Incensio

Releases no nectar

Perdition falls, jagged stone cold
The road to Mexicali
Is a mere eight miles
...or so I'm told

Gnawing thorn
Your spirit's torn
The cold nudge of the macabre may linger

But take heart
And fear naught
Saguaro simply gives you the finger.

SOULMATE
BY JOHN PHILLIPS

In the Guff
Where the souls are born
Spirits are twisted, torn in half
Cast down to Earth
In human form
Cursed for searching
Forevermore

But I laugh
Because in you I have found
An angel's mercy
Heaven bound
Surely my better half

About the Author

I have two beautiful children, Craig and Claire, a wonderful daughter-in-law, Marta, a wonderful son-in-law, Josh and also, two beautiful granddaughters, Mina and Aubrey. They are my life, my inspiration and my "personal cheerleaders." I come from a large family, have been raised in Dayton, Ohio, all of my life and have done some traveling. I have been writing as long as I can remember, love to read and am amazed about the endless creativity of people. Many teachers from my youth come to mind, as their encouragement has been unending. I am not sure of one specific thing that inspired me to write this book, although I have faith that the drive and spirit behind it, comes from the Divine, comes from the need to inspire others and also comes from the need to leave a legacy for my children.

About the Author
(Continued)

Once the bug for this book hit me, I was able to write these poems and narratives in a short amount of time. This project began on my birthday, in September of 2014, and ended promptly just weeks later, in early November. The majority of these thoughts and ideas came from a multitude of experiences, dreams and from loved ones. I am so happy to have wonderful life-long friends, and family, to support my journey along the way. I am truly blessed to have these people in my life and for them to allow me to be a part of their lives.

CPSIA information can be obtained
at www.ICGtesting.com
Printed in the USA
FFOW02n0711240216
21783FF